Linda Joy Singleton lives in northern California and often has strange encounters with playful cats, demanding dogs, and even pigs and horses. She has two grown children and a wonderfully supportive husband who loves to travel with her in search of unusual stories.

Linda Joy Singleton is the author of more than twenty-five books.

Visit Linda and other Llewellyn authors on the Web at:

teen.llewellyn.com

Shamrocked!

Linda Joy Singleton

Llewellyn Publications
St. Paul, Minnesota

FIRST EDITION
First printing, 2005

Book design and editing by Megan Atwood and Andrew Karre
Cover design by Ellen L. Dahl
Cover illustration © 2004 by Mike Harper/Artworks
Interior illustration by Ellen L. Dahl

Library of Congress Cataloging-in-Publication Data
Singleton, Linda Joy.
  Shamrocked! / Linda Joy Singleton — 1st ed.
    p. cm. — (Strange encounters)
  Summary: While staying at a Mount Shasta resort where her television host father is investigating sightings of a leprechaun, sixth-grader Cassie and her younger brother follow a map to a magical world where they learn about the meaning of friendship.
  ISBN: 0-7387-0594-2
    [1. Leprechauns — Fiction. 2. Maps — Fiction. 3. Magic — Fiction. 4. Friendship — Fiction. 5. Mount Shasta (Calif.) — Fiction.]
I. Title II. Series.

PZ7.S6177Sh 2005
[Fic] — dc22   2004048791

Llewellyn Publications
A Division of Llewellyn Worldwide, Ltd.
P.O. Box 64383, Dept. 0-7387-0594-2
St. Paul, MN 55164-0383, U.S.A.
www.llewellyn.com

Printed in the United States of America

Also from Linda Joy Singleton

To Lori Welch, in celebration of mystery games, coded messages, secret languages, cat clubs, square dancing, shared birthdays, and over thirty years of friendship. Best friends create real magic. I'm lucky to have a special friend like you.

Contents

prologue
Venting

Can you believe my terrible, rotten, stinky, awful bad luck?

I returned from a weekend so weird that I couldn't even tell my best friend Rosalie about it because:

a)   I made a promise, and

b)   She wouldn't believe me anyway.

So then what do I find out?

Rosalie has been having tons of fun—without me!

"I joined Club Glorious," she said, flipping her black ponytail like she'd become some kind of diva.

"There's tennis, miniature golf, an arcade, and three pools! The biggest pool is shaped like a whale with a slide that curves down the tail—and the lifeguard, Marc Lynburn, is *sooo* cool."

Marc is total coolness. But tennis, mini golf, and three pools are even *more* cool. So I begged my parents to join Club Glorious and—can you believe this?—they refused!

Dad said an elite club "discriminated against certain social and economic situations and separated a community rather than brought it together."

Whatever that means!

Mom said, "Why drive to a club for exercise and add to the air pollution? Ride your bike, or cool off in the sprinklers."

My brother wasn't any help either. Lucas only cared about these dumb acting classes he'd just started. And when my little sister, Amber, learned animals weren't allowed at Club Glorious, she ditched me to play in the sprinkler with her duck, Dribble.

So it was just me against my parents—and you can guess how that turned out.

But that wasn't the worst thing to happen. That came later with green goo, booby traps, and mysterious little people.

My bad luck had only just begun . . .

chapter one

Glorious
Gloom

Summer shone bright with cloudless skies, and sixth grade loomed two months and one week away. I'd been looking forward to sixth grade since kindergarten. No more being pushed around because I was one of the little kids. At last, I'd be a superior sixth grader.

Only, I came home from a weird weekend of camping and found out news that stunk worse than my brother's old socks and the tuna sandwich he left under his bed for a month. Ripe stinkola!

4

Due to overcrowding, the sixth graders would be shipped off to middle school. Instead of being a superior sixth on the playground, I'd be demoted to the bottom of the middle-school food chain. Seventh and eighth graders would rule and stray dogs would get more respect than sixth graders.

What had I done to deserve such BAD luck?

"Look on the bright side," Rosalie said as she stopped by on her way to Club Glorious. She had a towel draped over her shoulders, and her normally golden skin had tanned an even deeper golden-brown.

"What bright side?" I grumbled from my perch on our porch step, where I'd been sulking for hours.

"In another year, we'll be seventh graders and we can tease sixth graders."

"Don't stop there," I said sarcastically. "In a hundred years, we'll all be dead and dust and forgotten."

Rosalie just laughed. "I know what will cheer you up. I'll get a visitor's pass from Club Glorious, and you can come with me tomorrow."

"If my parents let me," I added with a groan.

"Keep asking till you wear them down." She glanced at her watch and gave a small squeal. "Oh! Marc is starting his lifeguard shift in five minutes. Talk to you later, Cassie." Then she dashed off for a date with a whale-shaped pool.

The shifting sun struck me in the face, and I went back inside.

From the kitchen, I heard Mom singing a country song off key and smelled pumpernickel bread. If Mom saw me looking bored, she'd make me eat something healthy. So I went to my bedroom and slammed the door behind me.

My summer is going to be the pits, I thought as I sank on my unmade bed. Everyone will be hanging out at Club Glorious, and I'll miss all the fun. What if Rosalie makes a new best friend? They'll swim and gossip together. They will start their own Glorious Girls Club, and all the girls will join. Except me.

More than anything, I wanted to be a Glorious Girl.

But the only way to join would be to pay for it myself, and I had less than ten dollars saved up. I needed money. A lot. Fast.

So I was sulking in my room, dreaming of winning lottery tickets, when there was a sharp *BANG!* on my door.

Only, when I opened it up, no one was there.

Just a letter lying on the floor.

Labeled "Treasure."

chapter two
Treasure Thief

"I took your treasure. Follow the map or lose your treasure forever."

I read the note again. What treasure? What map? Was this some kind of joke?

Okay Cassie, I told myself, think clearly to figure this out.

Cooling off under my ceiling fan, I perched on the edge of my bed and studied the note. Scrawled with black ink on lined paper, the printing was sloppy. Six-year-old Amber could do a neater job blindfolded, lefthanded, and hanging upside down. But then Amber was a neat freak. I mean, just look at her side of the room. Not a wrinkle on her bed-spread, no dust on her stuffed animals, and her dresser mirror sparkled with cleanliness.

(We will NOT talk about my side of the room.)

Treasure, I murmured as I sat back on my bed. But I don't have any gold doubloons, diamonds, or mountains of money, I thought. I wish!

The only unusual thing I owned was a zillofax, a gift from my very out-of-this-world friend, Vee. But my zillofax (it's a plastic briefcase that kids from Vee's planet use to carry homework) wasn't missing. It was where I left it, on the pile of dirty clothes by my closet. So what had been taken?

And then it hit me. Hard, right in the heart.

"Oh, no!" I jumped up. "Not Grandma's box!"

I hopped over my inline skates and yanked the handle of my bottom dresser drawer. Pushing aside pink, white, and blue bikini underwear, I searched for the precious carved wood box. My most special things were hidden inside Grandma's box, objects so SECRET no one else must ever see them.

The box had to be there.

Only it wasn't.

Where was it? *Where?* WHERE?

I started to tear my room apart when someone knocked on my door.

"It's not locked!" I called out, lying flat on my carpet and peering into the black pit beneath my bed. A whole lost civilization could be buried here, and I'd never see it through all the discarded food wrappers, forgotten homework assignments, and socks without mates.

Three more knocks on my door.

"JUST COME IN!" I shouted.

No answer, only another loud knock.

"This had better be important!" I stomped over to the door. It was probably Amber joking around. Or maybe Lucas the aspiring actor. Lately, he'd been a swashbuckling pirate, wearing an eye patch and waving a floppy plastic sword.

Grabbing the doorknob, I yanked it open—only no one was there. But when I looked on the ground, there was a single sheet of paper.

I picked it up, then puzzled over a crude drawing with strange penciled shapes, squiggly lines, and scribbled words.

It was a treasure map.

chapter three

A Frog, a Giraffe, and 13 Hands

I slipped on my sandals and then tucked my brown hair under a cap and set off in search of treasure.

Escaping the house without awkward questions was easy. Dad was miles away at his TV studio, working on this week's episode of *I Don't Believe It!* And Mom was in the kitchen baking for her Happy Planet Club meeting. Today, their topic was "The Joy of Composting."

But there was no escape from the blazing heat. How could I survive two more months without a swimming pool? Never happen! Already I was sweating enough to fill a lake. By the end of summer, there'd be nothing left of me except a puddle of soggy clothes and bones.

After a few blocks, I sat against a fire hydrant to study the map. What did the weird, uneven circles, triangles, and squiggly lines mean? Hmm . . . if the squiggly lines were streets and the circles were buildings, the cluster of triangles could be trees. A park? The nearest park was Glory Park, next to Club Glorious.

I sighed. I hated being left out. Right now, Rosalie was splashing in cool waves under the watchful gaze of Marc Lynburn. Most of the girls in my school were wild about him. Even me, though I'd never admit it—except, of course, to my Top-Secret Journal, which I'd hidden in Grandma's box.

"I have to get that box back!" I moaned.

More determined than ever, I studied the crudely drawn map. Confusing words squeezed together at the bottom of the paper: "giraffe + water, pass the jump frog, N 2 mouthwash, between clock 13."

"Huh? Weird code." I shook my head and nearly bumped into a street sign.

After pausing to check for traffic, I crossed into Glory Park. Walking under shady oaks and maple trees cooled my sticky skin. In the distance, I could see the impressive castlelike walls and the crown-shaped neon sign flashing "Club Glorious." A soft breeze teased me with faint smells of chlorine and coconut oil. Rosalie was probably lying on a chaise lounge while oh-so-cute Marc rubbed sunscreen on her.

A branch snapped behind me.

Whirling around, I glimpsed a flash of brown disappear behind dense bushes. Had someone been spying on me? Well they weren't going to get away with it!

I jammed the map in my pocket, then raced after the spy. Ducking under a low branch, I jogged around dense bushes until I came to a gravel road. I followed the road till it dead-ended at an overflowing trash bin. The only sign of life around was a squirrel peeking out of a ripped garbage bag.

A squirrel? Is that my spy? I wondered, feeling a bit silly. The sun was so hot that I was having a brain meltdown.

Back to searching for Grandma's box. My journal wasn't the only important thing I'd hidden inside. There was jewelry, like Great Aunt Margaret's opal ring, and an "I love you more than frogs" Valentine card I got in first grade from Nathan after I kissed him. (It was a dare, okay?) Also there's my foreign money collection. It's not worth much in US currency, but the German mark, Russian ruble, Italian lira, and Dutch guilder look really cool.

I kept walking until I came to a playground. I took a long drink from a fountain, then rested in the shade on a stone bench. Unfolding the map, I read through the clues. Then I read through them again. A giraffe, a frog, and mouthwash? Those were the dumbest clues ever. Where was I supposed to find a giraffe? The nearest zoo was over thirty miles away in Sacramento.

The map was a big joke—at my expense. Whoever made it was probably laughing at me right now.

Crumpling the map, I tossed it into a garbage can. "I give up!"

I turned around to leave.

Suddenly, there was a rustling sound behind me.

Then someone burst out the bushes and grabbed me.

chapter four
Map Quest

My attacker wore a pirate's costume, complete with a feather in the hat, an eye patch, and a fake sword stuck through his belt. He was "Strange" all right—Lucas Strange, my theatrically challenged brother.

"Cassie, you can't quit," he protested. "I worked hard on that map."

"It was you all along!" I pointed my finger at him. "You—you—you—THIEF!"

"Aye, dear sister, I admit me own guilt," he said, slipping into a bad pirate accent. "But 'twas for a higher cause. I plunder without malice, 'tis my trade, not thievery."

"Give me back my box!"

"The map will lead ye to your treasure."

"You call *that* a map? A blind monkey with broken arms could do better."

"'Tis not the fault of the map, but of the reader. Alas, I miscalculated your detection ability."

"Return my box right now, or I'm going to miscalculate you into little pieces!"

"Those who resort to violence possess but a feeble brain."

"Cut the fake accent. It's your clues that are feeble."

He dropped the accent. "My clues were brilliant." He glared at me, then plucked the wrinkled map from the garbage. "They were good enough to lead you to Glory Park. You could have figured it out if you hadn't given up. You were so close."

"How close?" I asked, wiping sweat from my forehead.

"You took a drink from the fountain—the fountain shaped like a giraffe."

"Huh?" I looked at the stone fountain. Long neck, tail, and a giraffe face. Lucas was right. The brat!

"See that springy toy on the playground?" Lucas gestured with his fake sword. "It's a green jumping frog. And 'N 2' obviously means to go 'north to' the treasure. And what's the most popular mouthwash?"

"I don't—oh . . ." A TV jingle popped into my head: *Fresh as summer showers, with germ killing powers. Gargle, swoosh, and spit: Red Rose Mouthwash, a refreshing hit!*

Lucas led me past the playground, to a rose garden.

Okay, I felt like a total doofus. But I wasn't about to admit that to my brother. I hated it when he showed off his high IQ. He was a year younger, yet because he was in the "gifted" program, we'd be starting sixth grade together.

"Okay, Einstein. What about the clock?" I faced him with my hands on my hips. "There's no such thing as a clock that goes to thirteen."

"But if you continue north from the rose garden, what do you see?"

I didn't want to look, but I did anyway. It's not like it was even a real clock—just a decorative clock strung together with colored rocks in a circle on the ground. Two wooden arrows pointed the time. The big arrow aimed at the one and the little arrow on the three.

One-three. Thirteen.

I groaned.

"Between the one and three is number two." Lucas lifted up the large rock marking the "two" spot. There, in a small hole, was my "treasure." He handed it to me with an I'm-smarter-than-you smile.

"Nothing had better be missing," I warned as I lifted the lid to check.

"I wouldn't take your dumb stuff," he said defensively. "I made up the game so I could improve my acting skills. Ms. Bennett says I have natural talent."

"Ms. Bennett?"

"My acting teacher—at least she *was* my teacher."
He frowned. "I told Mom and Dad I wasn't allowed to
miss any lessons. But they wouldn't listen and just
ordered me to pack."

"Pack?" I almost dropped my box. "What are you
talking about?"

"Didn't they tell you?"

"Tell me what?"

"About the trip we're taking tomorrow."

"Trip? Tomorrow?" An ugly suspicion wormed
its way into my head. "Does this has something to
do with Dad's show?"

"Yes." The feather on his Lucas' hat bobbed as he
nodded. "Dad's taking us to the mountains. To hunt
for leprechauns."

chapter five

Pot of Gold Fever

Leprechauns? I puzzled as I raced home. But leprechauns aren't real. They're pretend, like fairies and dragons. You can't find a pot of gold at the end of a rainbow, and little people don't grant wishes.

Of course, little green aliens weren't supposed to exist either. My alien friend Vee was silver, not green, and she definitely did exist. But I was the only one who met her—except for Amber. And Amber's memories of our strange adventure had been erased. Or had they? Since the campout, my sister had been sneaking around like she had a secret.

When I arrived home, I found the living room full of Happy Planet Club members. Everyone was listening to Mom as she talked about a new petition to save a rare species of worm. Mom was big on petitions, although it seemed like a waste of time to me.

Dad usually came home for lunch, and I found him in the kitchen. Bursting through the door, I put my hands on my hips and demanded, "Is it true?"

He set down his grilled goat-cheese sandwich and looked up at me with an amused twinkle in his gray eyes. "Is what true?"

"Lucas just told me," I said accusingly. "About hunting for leprechauns."

"You can't hunt for something that isn't real," Dad said with a chuckle. "But you can hunt for the truth behind wild stories. There have been several leprechaun sightings in Mount Shasta. It's a hoax, of course, and I'll prove it to my viewers."

"So we're really going on another trip?"

"That's right. We can't leave you kids with your grandparents since they're still touring Europe. So the whole family is going. Get busy packing, because we're leaving bright and early tomorrow morning."

"But—but I can't! I wanted to go with Rosalie tomorrow. She's getting me a free pass to Club Glorious."

"Sorry, hon," he said reaching out to pat my hand. "You'll have to go with her another time. I've already made the reservations, and I'm on a tight schedule."

"It's not fair!" I glared at the man who was ruining my life. "Can't I stay with Rosalie?"

Dad tapped his finger to his chin, as if considering this. "If you really don't want to go on this trip, I won't force you."

"Thanks! You're the greatest." I jumped up. "I'll call Rosalie right—"

"Not so fast." Dad put up his hand. "First, I'll need to discuss this with your mother. Then, if she agrees, you may spend the next few days with Rosalie's family. Although I'm surprised you'd want to."

"Why?"

"I was sure you'd be excited to go on this trip."

An odd tone in his voice set off my curiosity. I could tell he was waiting for me to ask more questions. But I stubbornly pursed my mouth shut.

I so do *not* want to go hunting leprechauns, I thought. Even if they're real, it's not like they'll offer me gold or wishes. And aren't they supposed to be in Ireland? So what are they doing in California?

There was a long pause, with Dad staring up at me and me trying to look away. Finally, I gave in and asked, "Oh, all right. Why would I want to go?"

"Because the Golden Shamrock Resort offers wonderful luxuries."

"Resort? Luxuries?" My hopes perked up. Our last family trip had meant roughing it in the wilderness without electricity and running water. I'd ended up having fun, but a girl could always do with a few luxuries.

Dad went on to describe king-size beds in huge rooms with hot tubs, room service, a zillion TV channels, a heated swimming pool, tennis courts, hiking trails, miniature golf course, a gym, and an arcade.

When he'd finished talking, I was hooked—maybe even drooling a little. Golden Shamrock Resort sounded way better than Club Glorious.

Rosalie was going to turn green with envy!

I raced to the phone to call her.

chapter six
Amber's Secret

It was a *looong* drive up Interstate 5 to Mount Shasta. And no fun at all because Lucas was a grump. Was it my fault he was missing his acting class? He refused to talk and stonily read a play called *A Midsummer Night's Dream*.

Amber wasn't any company either. She'd buckled herself in the seat behind me and announced, "I'm playing secret fort." Then she ducked under a blanket.

After fifty brain-boring miles of nothing to do and no one to talk to, I nudged Lucas. "Want to play car bingo?"

My brother didn't look up from his stupid acting book.

"How about license tag?"

He flipped to a new page, totally ignoring me.

"I'll let you go first," I offered.

Still no response.

"You can go first *and* count our California license plate."

He closed his book and adjusted the feather in his pirate hat. "Well . . . okay. Only the most dastardly pirate would ignore the pleas of a damsel in distress." Then he pointed out the window at a semi truck. "Alabama! Two points to zero!"

An hour later, the scenery had changed from golden fields to forest-green hills, and I was rapidly losing the war of the states. Nineteen to four! Can you believe Lucas even found a Hawaii license? Like, how did a car from Hawaii get here? Swim?

I was ready to wave a white flag and surrender. Hoping maybe Amber could help, I twisted around in my seatbelt to talk to her. But my words froze in my mouth when I saw a long furry tail poking out from her blanket.

It wasn't like any tail I'd ever seen. Silky fur swirled with kaleidoscope colors. My first thought was that it must be a toy—until it rumbled with a musical purr. Then it flipped over and a large purple eye blinked at me.

The tail was alive!

Suddenly everything made sense—Amber's sneaky behavior, the way she hid under the blanket, the musical purring sound. My sweet little sister had smuggled an alien creature off Vee's spaceship! She probably didn't even know it was from another planet. But she was smart enough to hide it—and sneaky enough to keep her secret.

Just what I didn't need on my luxury resort vacation! And the worst thing was that I couldn't tell anyone.

Amber's secret had become my secret, too.

chapter seven
Bad Luck
Resort

My alien friend kept a hidden room filled with bizarre creatures on her spaceship. I'd never seen them, but Vee told me about *snogards, katahsies,* and *goofinks*. Amber's big-eyed creature couldn't be a snogard, because it didn't have a shaggy beard oozing with slimy black bugs. And katahsies had big ears that flapped out like wings. So this must be a goofink, I guessed.

Vee said goofinks were playful and cuddly, which didn't sound dangerous. But alien pets belonged with aliens—not a softhearted human. I had to warn

Amber before something scary happened. Only, how in the world could I convince my sister that her new pet was from another planet?

"Here's our turn-off!" Dad called out.

I looked up as Dad turned down a narrow ribbon of road twisting through dense forest. Even with the window shut, I could smell the fragrant scent of pine. Despite my worries about Amber and the goofink, my heart jumped with excitement. Fancy room, heated pool, and luxury living—here I come!

I pressed my face against the window, eager for my first glimpse of Golden Shamrock Resort. But the road kept on and on, curving and climbing for miles, until we made a sharp right turn at a fancy carved wooden sign shaped like a shamrock.

"We're here!" Dad rang out.

"At last!" I tugged on Lucas's shirt. "What do you want to do first? Play tennis, miniature golf, arcade games, or swim?"

"I'd rather have acting lessons," he grumbled as he looked up from a magazine called *Child Star Quarterly*.

"Stop being a grump." I punched his arm.

"I can't help it. I'm missing auditions for our first play. Ms. Bennett brags that her most successful student, Trevor Tremaine, never missed a class. Now he's the star of the Chuckle Cookie commercials."

"That cute blond kid with the funny laugh?"

"Trevor isn't really blond, that's a wig. I want to be successful like him."

"Missing one lesson won't matter. You're the best actor I know."

"You really think so?"

"Well, duh!" I looked him straight in the eye. "And you're going to have fun on this trip even if you don't want to."

"Well . . . I do like tennis."

"And I can't wait to swim. The brochure said the pool was shaped like a shamrock."

"Cool." Lucas rolled up his magazine and tucked it into his pocket. "If there's a diving board, I'll be a pirate, and you can have the role of the captured damsel being forced to walk the plank."

I rolled my eyes and tactfully avoided any sarcastic comments.

The road changed from pavement to rough dirt, and the car lurched over potholes. Lucas bumped into me; then I slammed into him. Behind me, I heard a shrill, alien squeak. Was the goofink squeamish? I hoped it wouldn't goo-upchuck.

Stone and wood buildings rose into view. A beautifully landscaped courtyard led to the largest building, which rose high into three stories of rustic wood, river rocks, with stained-glass windows and elegant balconies. Classy! Stone leprechauns decorated a grassy front yard. There were other, smaller buildings beyond the main resort. I couldn't see a pool, but it was probably enclosed behind the chainlink gate beyond the resort.

A tall woman with ice-blue hair and a gentle smile bustled out to greet us. She wore a yellow satin blouse, plaid skirt, and gold shamrock earrings that sparkled in the sun.

"Welcome, welcome! I am Agathena Truelock." Instead of holding out her hand, though, she lifted the edges of her skirt and curtsied—like she was greeting royalty. "I'm honored to meet you, Mr. Strange."

"The honor is mine, Mrs. Truelock. And call me Jonathan," Dad said, slipping into his smiling TV-personality mode. "This is my wife Katherine, my son Lucas, and my oldest daughter Cassie. My youngest, Amber, must be asleep in the van."

"It's so exciting to have a famous celebrity staying here," Mrs. Truelock gushed. "I have every episode of your show on tape. That exposé on Frankenstein's dog was incredible. I do so love how you always end with 'And that's why I don't believe it.' Gives me goosebumps every time I hear it."

"Oh brother," my brother grumbled. "Another groupie."

"She seems nice," I told him.

"They all do before they start sending sicko letters to Dad. The worst was that pink-haired lady who snuck into our house and stole Dad's socks."

"Right out of the hamper. *Pee-yew!*" I giggled. "Boy was she shocked when Dribble turned into an attack duck and chased her away."

Lucas laughed. "Amber has some weird pets."

"That's for sure." I glanced uneasily at the back of our van and wondered if the Golden Shamrock Resort had a "No Alien Pet" rule.

I followed as Mrs. Truelock led my parents to the office. They were all smiling and talking about boring adult stuff. I didn't pay much attention until I heard Mrs. Truelock say "I do hope the children won't mind."

"Of course they won't," Mom assured politely.

"Won't mind what?" I asked, hurrying to catch up.

Dad patted me on the head like an obedient pet. "Our kids will be happy wherever you put them."

"Such lovely children—as charming as their father," Mrs. Truelock said in a syrupy voice. "I'm so relieved they won't mind a few inconveniences."

"Inconveniences?" I stopped right in front of them so they had to stop too. "What do you mean?"

"We've had a few problems lately." Mrs. Truelock laughed nervously. "It's why I contacted your father in the first place."

"The leprechaun," I muttered.

"Pesky little fellow." She sighed. "His idea of fun is hurting business. My husband is still limping after a falling into a booby-trapped hole, and the green slime clogged up our plumbing something awful."

"You've seen this leprechaun?" Dad asked. His tone was casual, but his gray eyes glinted with interest.

"Yes. My husband has, too." She waved her hand. "But we can discuss that later. You must be tired after your long drive. Many of our rooms are being repaired, but I have a lovely third-floor suite for you and your wife. It has every comfort—kitchenette, balcony, large-screen TV, and a private hot tub."

"My own kitchen!" Mom looked excited. "I'll be able to make the kids healthy meals. Wonderful!"

"Not as wonderful as I'd hoped," Mrs. Truelock said in a regretful tone. "I was going to have your children stay in the suite adjoining your room. Unfortunately, my husband assigned it to another family this morning."

Lucas and I exchanged worried looks.

"So where are we staying?" I demanded.

"Out in the barn."

chapter eight
Stalled

It really was a barn. Or at least it had been about a hundred years ago. Now there were colorful rugs on the wood floor and painted white walls, but a whiff of cow still lingered. We each had our own stall—I mean, bedroom—with a twin-size bed, dresser, lamp, and small desk. Instead of a modern bathroom, we would have to tromp outside around the back to an outhouse. I couldn't believe it! Not again!

"Check out this rope!" Lucas exclaimed. "Reminds me of an old Errol Flynn movie. You know, pirates swinging from ropes and having sword fights. Bet Mr. Perfect Actor Trevor never stayed in a barn."

"Lucky guy." I picked up a piece of hay from a rug.

"There could be a pirate chest in that loft. Climb up with me."

"No way," I said in a foul mood.

"Now who's being a grump?"

"Don't you even care that we're stuck here like livestock?"

"No. This place is cool." He had climbed halfway up the rope, and I was getting dizzy watching him sway back and forth. "It'll be fun to explore. A barn is way better a regular room."

"We don't have a TV, hot tub, or even a real bathroom."

"So what? I like it, and you don't hear Amber complaining."

"That's because Amber has a—" I slapped my hand over my mouth.

"Huh?" Lucas peered down from the hayloft. "What does Amber have?"

"A big imagination." I plucked another piece of hay from the carpet and twisted it while I forced myself to sound casual. "Amber doesn't care about anything real. She's probably pretending her stall is a magical castle. But *I* know the awful reality. Is it too much to ask for just a little luxury?"

Lucas slid down the rope and stirred up dust when he plopped on the wood floor. He whipped out a red scarf from his pocket and tied it around his head, pirate style. "Fear not, dispirited maiden. I shall come to your aid with a pleasurable diversion. Be quick to don your bathing apparel, and we'll journey off to yonder pool."

"The pool?" I asked hopefully. "You'll go swimming with me?"

"Aye. 'Tis that not what I just said?"

"With you, it's hard to tell—but thanks."

Mom would get on my case if I didn't invite Amber, so I knocked on her door. There was a bang and a squeak. Then Amber shouted for me to go away. I knew what she was hiding, and she would have to know I knew—eventually.

But first, I had a date with a shamrock-shaped pool.

My swimming suit had been a birthday gift when I turned eleven last April. It was a green-striped two piece with gold trim. There was just enough padding you-know-where to give me curves so I didn't look like a badly drawn stick figure. And when I slipped it on, I knew I looked good.

Lucas and I walked on the bricked path bordering the main building. When the bricks ended, the ground became rocky and overgrown with weeds. A prickly weed spiked through my sandal, and I paused to yank it out. Then I hurried to catch up with Lucas.

"There's the pool!" I pointed toward a glint of water surrounded by a chainlink fence. "Last one in is a piranha!"

"That'll be you, fish-face," Lucas retorted.

We both started running, and I was in the lead— almost to the gate—when I stubbed my toe and pitched forward.

Plop! I found myself lying on my stomach. As I pushed myself up, I heard an odd rustling sound above me. Tilting my head back, I stared up into a towering, twisted old pine. Something moved in the tree. Not some*thing*, but some*one*. A scrawny, brown-haired boy in a leather jacket and red T-shirt. His black cowboy boots dangled high above the ground as he grinned and waved at me.

"Lucas!" I called over to my brother. "Look!"

He followed my gaze. "At what?"

"In that tree!"

My brother shook his head. "I don't see anything."

"Huh?" I blinked. "But he was . . . I saw him . . . Where'd he go?"

"Who?"

"A boy—smaller than you, but older, I think." I shook my head in puzzlement. "He was sitting on that tree branch."

"Way up there? I'm a good climber, but I'd need wings to get that high." Lucas playfully punched my shoulder. "I bet you think he's a leprechaun."

"No way!"

"Good, because Dad says they don't exist."

"I know." But I really wasn't sure. Dad hadn't thought aliens existed either.

Lucas jumped and started to run. "Beat you to the pool!"

I brushed dirt off my shorts, then followed my brother. Only I couldn't go very fast in floppy sandals.

"Hey, Cassie! You were right." Lucas opened the gate. "The pool is shaped like a shamrock—and it's colored green. I'm going for the diving board. Watch me!"

Lucas climbed up a ladder and sprinted across the diving board. Then he arched with perfect dive and splashed into the water.

Immediately, Lucas popped up with an ear-shattering scream.

"HELP!" He flailed his arms. "They're after me!"

"What?" I shouted.

"PIRANHAS!"

chapter nine

Courting
Trouble

Hundreds of fish! Maybe thousands!

Dark, swishing shapes swarmed all around my brother like the dinner bell had rung and Lucas was the main course. Screaming in panic, he splashed and kicked wildly, floundering in murky green water.

I couldn't just stand by and watch my brother be eaten by a pack of hungry piranhas. But what could I do? If I left to get help, by the time I got back Lucas could be a chewed-up, bloody pulp. Yet, if I jumped in, I'd be attacked, too—and my new swimsuit would be ruined.

Running around the pool, I looked for a life preserver or some kind of weapon to fight biting fish. But I only found a heavy coil of rope. It was better than nothing.

With Lucas's cries ringing in my ears, I pushed the rope to the edge of the pool. As I bent over, a dark shadow wiggled to the surface. The gray-black fish was long and chubby, with beady black eyes and whiskers.

Whiskers? I thought. But piranhas don't have whiskers.

And then it hit me—right in the funny bone.

"Lucas, you guppy brain." I dropped the rope and burst into laughter. "They aren't piranhas."

"Huh?" He stopped screaming. "They—they aren't?"

"Not even close."

"Then what are they?"

"Catfish."

"Are you sure?" Treading water, he looked down. "They won't hurt me?"

"Not unless you're a mousefish."

He glared. "You think this is funny?"

"Definitely."

"You aren't so brave either." Lucas swam to the side of the pool. "I don't see you jumping in for a swim."

"And you won't ever," I said firmly. "Swimming with fish is fine in the ocean or a lake, but not in a gross pool. Haven't they ever heard of chlorine? Yuck!"

"This isn't a pool—it's an aquarium." Lucas grabbed his towel, shivering as he dried off. "And the pool isn't heated either. *Brrr!*"

Did the boy in the tree have anything to do with this? I wondered. But how could a little kid fill a huge pool with hundreds of fish?

We decided to tell Mrs. Truelock. We found her outside the front office watering flowers. When we told her about the pool, she dropped her watering can and burst into tears.

"Not the pool, too!" she cried, covering her face with her hands. "When will it all end? I can't take any more bad news."

Lucas and I stared at each other in dismay.

I didn't know what to say, so I just mumbled, "I'm sorry."

"It's not your fault. It's that horrid prankster."

"Dad will stop him," Lucas said loyally.

"If anyone can, it's your father. I thank my stars he's come to help me. The prankster is ruining everything. And I feel bad that you dear children had such a terrible start to your vacation."

"The fish didn't hurt me," Lucas said.

"But now you won't be able to go swimming. It'll take days for my husband to clean the pool."

"We don't need to swim," I assured. She was a nice lady, and I wanted to make her feel better.

Mrs. Truelock wiped her tears away and gave a faint smile. "Thank you for being so understanding."

"Don't worry. We'll find something else to do."

"We like tennis," Lucas added. "Where's the tennis court?"

Mrs. Truelock gave us a funny look, then hurried into her office. Minutes later she returned carrying a large cardboard box.

"Everything you need is in here," she told us.

"What?" Both Lucas and I asked in confusion.

"Equipment for tennis, croquet, miniature golf, horseshoes, and more." She handed the box to Lucas. "Why don't you invite our other young guest to join you."

"A skinny boy wearing black boots?" I guessed.

"I didn't notice what he was wearing, but his family is staying in the suite next to your parents."

The luxurious room we were supposed to have, I thought enviously. No wonder he was grinning at me. The room thief!

Lucas frowned at the box. "So where are the tennis courts?"

"Wherever you decide to set up." Mrs. Truelock waved her hand. "Choose some place away from the trees, though. We lose more balls that way."

Then she picked up her watering can and went into the front office.

"So now what?" I said, my hopes sinking fast. I felt sorry for Mrs. Truelock, but I felt worse for me. Nothing was turning out like I hoped. No fancy rooms, swimming pool, or tennis courts. I wished I'd stayed with Rosalie.

"We could go cat-fishing," Lucas joked.

I glared at him. "I heard little brothers make good bait."

"Or we could play tennis," he added quickly.

I shrugged. "It's better than nothing."

While Lucas scouted ahead for a clearing, I went to see if Amber wanted to join us. But her door was still locked. And when I knocked, she shouted, "Go away!"

So I did.

A few minutes later I found Lucas in a clearing next to a dense grove of trees.

"Welcome to the tennis court." Lucas plopped the game box on the dirt and gave an exaggerated sweep on his arm. "Open air with a fresh smell of pine."

"And no waiting in line for a court," I said, trying to be a good sport.

"Hey, check out all the stuff."

I poked through the box, amazed so much was squeezed inside. Board games, tennis balls, plastic poles and a net, a flat volleyball, horseshoes, darts, marbles, a Ping-Pong paddle, a baseball bat (but no ball), a ripped catcher's mitt, and a glow-in-the-dark Frisbee.

"There's only one tennis racket," Lucas said, disappointed.

"And one Ping-Pong paddle," I added.

So we improvised. Lucas played with the tennis racket, and I smacked the ball with a Ping-Pong paddle. Or at least I tried to. Mostly I missed the ball.

"I hereby rename our game," I said, running back to serve, "Chase the Ball."

"Don't aim for my leg this time," he joked.

"I'm lucky to hit the ball at all with this small paddle!"

I swung back and *WHACK!* My ball streaked right for Lucas's face. He ducked just in time, swinging his racket wildly and sending the ball flying high over my head. It crashed into a clump of manzanita. Groaning, I chased after another ball.

After getting scratched searching through prickly manzanita, I spotted the ball under a twisted red branch. I reached out, only the ball rolled away.

"Weird," I murmured.

"Stop playing with the ball," Lucas called.

"I'm not—it's playing with me!" The ball zig-zagged out of reach. Was it remote controlled or a trick ball?

Just as my hand closed over it, there was a whooshing sound. Looking up, I saw a round pink missile flying toward me.

SPLAT! Water spilled down on my head.

"What the—" I stared in astonishment at a cloud of blue, red, green, pink, and yellow balloons. An air fleet of water bombs.

"Lucas! Look out!" I covered my head with my hands. "We're being attacked!"

chapter ten
Bombs Away

Plop! Plop! Splash!

Spiraling rainbow water bombs rained down like meteors. Where were they coming from and who was throwing them? I tried to look, but the balloons were coming too fast.

"I'm gonna get whoever is doing this!" Lucas wiped his face, then raised an angry fist. "Cassie, let's go find him!"

"He's somewhere in those trees!" I pointed to a thick grove of pines.

Soggy hair dangled in my eyes. Another balloon crashed at my feet. The attack didn't let up until we neared the trees. Then, suddenly, it stopped.

"The bomber has to be close," Lucas said as he wrung out his dripping T-shirt.

"But where?" I checked behind a gnarled tree trunk. "No one here."

"Maybe in those bushes." He pointed to some berry bushes.

But all we found were thorns and unripe berries.

"He's got to be here," Lucas said.

"But where?" I slumped on a mossy stump. "I don't see anyone."

"Can't see me?" a high-pitched voice rang out. "Try in the tree!"

I peered up into a towering pine. The brown-haired boy I'd seen earlier sat on a crooked branch, holding a cloth bag. He reached in the bag and pulled out an orange balloon.

"You!" I waved my fist at him. "You little creep!"

"I may be little, but you're all wet." His cowboy boots swayed back and forth as he chuckled.

"You're gonna be worse when we get a hold of you!" Lucas lunged at the tree trunk and started to climb.

"I'm *soooo* scared." The boy raised a blue balloon. "Catch!"

The balloon sailed toward Lucas. My brother leaped high and caught the balloon without breaking it.

The boy applauded. "Neato mosquito! Great catch!"

Lucas drew back his arm and hurled the water bomb at the boy. The balloon whizzed through the branches and whooshed over the boy's head.

"Missed me, missed me!" The boy laughed so hard, he lost his balance. Kicking wildly, his arms flailed, and he tried to grab a branch. Only it snapped. A scream, branches cracking, pine needles showering like prickly rain, then the boy was lying on the ground. Still as death.

Rushing over, I knelt down by his side. "Are you okay?"

He gave out a raspy moan.

"Lucas!" I cried. "We need to get him to a doctor!"

"Or leave him as a snack for a hungry bear."

I glared at my brother. "How can you be so heartless?"

"Because I know a fake when I see one. And this little creep is a big fake. His breathing is too even, and he's not even bleeding."

"Of course he's hurt! He fell at least twenty feet." I looked up and couldn't even see the sky through the thick trees. "I think he's staying in the suite next to Mom and Dad's. I'll watch him while you get help."

"Listen to your sister." The boy weakly lifted his head. "I could be dying here."

"You could be, but you're not." Lucas put his hands on his hips. "At least give a good performance."

"If you insist." He suddenly arched his back and flipped forward to land on his feet. "I'll go back in the tree and fall again."

"What?" I exclaimed, relief switching to anger. "You were faking!"

"I knew it." Lucas snapped his fingers. "But why?"

"Nothing else to do." He shrugged. "It's boring-smoring around here."

"Why attack us?" I demanded. "We never did anything to you."

"Well, you should. I got you all wet, so you should hate me."

I shook my head. "I don't know you well enough to hate you."

"I'm Hank. Introduction over—now smack a balloon at me. I deserve it."

He did deserve it, but it felt wrong to attack him. Especially since he was younger than me—or was he? Although small and slim, Hank seemed mature. And his triangular face framed amazing chameleon eyes that changed color from green to brown to gold.

While I stood there trying to decide what to do, Lucas picked up a red water balloon and hurled it at Hank.

Splash! Water dribbled down Hank's face. But the goofy kid just laughed.

"Now that was fun!" Hank said. "Do it again!"

"I should," Lucas said, his sneakers sloshing as he moved. "I'm totally soaked."

"Yeppers. You're a soggy mess because of me. Everyone says I'm terrible, and I am. So go ahead." He spread out his arms like a human target. "Splash me again."

Lucas's arm wavered as he raised another balloon—then slowly came down. "I can't. It's no fun when you want me to."

"Exactly!" Hank grinned. "Oh, I do like your attitude. Finally some interesting friends. Hang around and we'll have more fun."

Was he joking or crazy? I was still angry because of the water bombs, but I was curious, too. "How old are you?" I asked.

"Old enough for everything."

"Me, too." Lucas grinned. "By the way, I'm Lucas and this is my sister, Cassie. We'll be at the resort for a few days. How about you?"

"Longer. I like it so much, I may never go home."

"I don't blame you," I said a bit enviously. "Your suite must be really nice."

He grinned like I'd told a funny joke. "The best I ever stayed in."

"Ours is better." Lucas pointed toward the barn. "Wait till you see it, Hank. There's a climbing rope and the hayloft is like a big raised stage. Perfect for a thespian like me."

I rolled my eyes and thought, here Lucas goes again, bragging about his acting. Only, most kids don't know what he's talking about and think a "thespian" is a breed of monkey or a contagious disease. Not Hank, though.

"You're an actor?" Hank asked.

"I was born to perform." Lucas nodded proudly. "Someday I'll be famous."

"Neato mosquito!" Hank's face lit up. "Let's put on a play!"

"There's no time," Lucas said with a glance at his watch. "Mom wants us back for lunch at noon. Hey, why don't you come with us?"

"You really want me to?" Hank asked in disbelief.

"Sure. If you're brave enough to eat food that's good for you and looks weird. Mom's a health-food freak. But her soy burgers are okay."

"And her broccoli-chip cookies are actually yummy," I added.

"Why are you being so nice to me?" Hank looked down at his boots. "I was mean and soaked you with water balloons."

"I threw one back." Lucas grinned. "Even if I missed."

"It was a good throw. Next time I'll stand still so you can soak me good."

Lucas laughed, and I even smiled a little. Okay, so maybe Hank wasn't a creep. Sure, he was a weird, but weird was normal for my family.

As we took down the tennis net, Lucas asked Hank, "Have you heard about the pranks?"

"Yeppers." His eyes twinkled green like pine needles. "But I only got here this morning, so I missed all the action."

"You didn't miss much," Lucas said with a grimace. "I may never jump into a pool again, though."

"At least not without checking for piranhas," I joked.

"Piranhas?" Hank asked. "I didn't hear about that, but I saw a toilet on the second floor oozing green slime. Any idea who did it?"

"Mrs. Truelock thinks it's a leprechaun," Lucas said with the same skeptical look Dad gets when he's investigating a wild story.

"Unbelievable!" Hank exclaimed. "Leprechauns don't exist."

"Yeah, it's probably some kid playing jokes."

"But it's no joke," I told them. "Mrs. Truelock is really upset, and I wish I could do something to help her. The prankster is ruining her business. He needs to be stopped."

But Lucas and Hank weren't listening. They were sorting through the game box, joking over missing equipment and broken games.

That familiar left-out feeling returned. And I missed Rosalie more than ever. Her family once spent a vacation at a circus camp, and she got a lot of great ideas for games—like tightrope walking across a fence or balancing empty milk cartons on our heads. We always had a great time together.

Wonder if Rosalie misses me, too, I thought. Or is she too busy splashing around with the Glorious Girls?

Hearing voices, I saw two people heading our way. Mrs. Truelock's flowing plaid skirt billowed with her quick strides. A small figure hurried beside her.

"Yoo-hoo!" Mrs. Truelock called out. "Cassie! Lucas!"

"Wonder what she wants." Lucas lifted his head. "And who's the kid? He's looks familiar."

"I can't tell from this far," I said. "Maybe Hank knows."

But when I turned to ask Hank, he wasn't there. He had disappeared.

chapter eleven
Star Struck

There wasn't time to look for Hank, because Lucas suddenly recognized the brown-haired boy with Mrs. Truelock.

"No way!" Lucas grasped my arm in panic. "It can't be him!"

"Him who?"

Lucas's face drained of color and his mouth moved but no sounds came out.

"Yoo-hoo!" Mrs. Truelock waved cheerily as she neared us. "Cassie, Lucas!"

The boy was a few years older than Amber—round and cute like a teddy bear. His navy jeans, sneakers, and blue polo shirt looked neat and expensive.

He seemed to notice I was staring. He said "Hi" and waved indifferently.

I'd never met him before, but the feeling of knowing him was strong—like I'd seen his face many times. Knew his voice. Heard his laugh . . .

That was it!

"You're the Chuckle Cookie kid!" Then I slapped my hand over my mouth before I said anything else lame.

"Trevor Tremaine," Lucas whispered in awe.

"I've dropped the 'Tremaine'," the boy said as he joined us. "It's just Trevor now."

"Trevor, I'd like you to meet Cassie and Lucas Strange," Mrs. Truelock said in a rush. "I'm sure you'll get along famously. I have to hurry for an appointment with the plumber. You children enjoy yourselves." Then she left.

We were silent for a moment. Lucas stared at Trevor, awestruck and tongue-tied. Trevor kicked at the dirt, like he wasn't happy being stuck with us.

I finally broke the ice. "Lucas is an actor, too."

"Oh?" Trevor turned to my brother. "Who represents you?"

"My parents, I guess."

"What roles have you played?"

"Well . . ." Lucas gnawed his lower lip. "I was a giraffe in our last school play."

"A dancing giraffe," I added proudly. "And he got a standing ovation."

Trevor stared at us like we were speaking another language.

"I'm studying with Ms. Bennett," Lucas said. "She says you were her best student, and she has pictures of you in her studio."

"Oh, nice." Trevor sounded distracted. "So what do we do here for fun?"

"Play tennis." I held up my Ping-Pong paddle. "Sort of."

"I heard you were up for a role in that soap opera, *Stormy Days and Nights,*" Lucas said. "Did you get it?"

"My manager decided it wasn't a big enough part." Trevor kicked at a weed. "We're in talks with several major studios for movie roles."

"Wow! You must be really excited."

"Not especially." Trevor shrugged. "It's just another job."

"Will you be acting with any famous stars?"

"Of course. But I can't talk about it yet."

"I understand," my brother said humbly.

But I didn't understand why an actor waiting to hear about important movie roles was here in Mount Shasta. And I didn't like how Trevor brushed off my brother.

"So what brings you here, Trevor?" I asked. "This isn't exactly Hollywood."

"My parents wanted me to have just a few days of rest," he explained. "You simply have no idea what it's like having fans following you everywhere, snapping pictures, begging for autographs. For a few days, I'm an average kid on vacation. Just like you."

I wanted to slap that smug smile off his "famous" face. "But we're *not* on vacation. Our father is working on a story for his cable *TV show.*"

Talk about a change of attitude. My words were a zap of lightning that sparked Trevor's interest. "TV show?" he echoed.

"Yes." I smiled. "But it's just another job."

"Did you say your last name was Strange? You mean your father is *the* Jonathan Strange—the creator and star of *I Don't Believe It!?*"

"That's our dad," I answered.

"Cool! His show gets great ratings, and he knows everyone who matters."

"Like us," I said sarcastically.

Trevor ignored me and turned to Lucas. "So you're in Ms. Bennett's class?"

"Yeah." Lucas smiled shyly. "But I'm just starting out."

"Don't be modest! I can tell you have loads of talent. Come to my room and I'll show you some scripts I'm considering."

"Scripts? Like for real movies? Wow!"

They hurried away, leaving me alone with a box of mismatched games.

Being a thespian *is* a disease, I thought in annoyance. And my brother has it bad.

chapter twelve

Hair Today,
Gone Tomorrow

Lunch à la Mom consisted of:

- Soy burgers with goat cheese
- Sliced organic pickles
- Wheat-germ chips
- Green-tomato juice
- Carob pudding

Mom didn't mind that Lucas was having lunch with a new friend, but she did mind that Amber hadn't showed up.

"Where's your sister?" Mom poured me a glass of green-tomato juice. "I haven't seen her since about an hour ago when she borrowed my hairbrush."

"Why would she borrow yours?" I asked. "She has one of her own."

"She forgot to pack hers."

I raised an eyebrow. Amber was neat and organized like Mom, and she never forgot anything. Did this have something to do with the goofink?

"I'll go get Amber," I offered quickly, not wanting Mom to walk in on Amber playing with an alien pet.

As I neared my sister's stall/room, I heard music. Where had my sister gotten a radio? She hadn't packed a boom box—but I had. And I'd left it in my room.

"Amber!" I banged on her door. "Open up!"

Instantly, the music stopped, and I heard footsteps.

"Hi, Cassie." Amber only opened the door a crack. "What do you want?"

"My boom box. Do you have it?"

"No."

Her tone screamed guilt. Also, she looked a mess. Her golden hair was tangled and there was a scratch on her chin. I pushed the door open a little wider. Neat-freak Amber hadn't made her bed or put away her clothes! For the first time in history, her room was messier than mine.

"What's going on?" I demanded.

"Nothing."

"So you won't mind if I search your room?"

"No! Don't!"

She tried to shut her door, but I stuck my foot in the way and pushed into her room. "I know I heard music in here."

"But it wasn't your boom box!" she protested. "It was—It was—"

"What?" A new suspicion crept into my mind. "Where did the music come from?"

"I can't tell you."

"But I can tell you," I said more gently. "I know you have a goofink."

"Goo . . . *what?*"

"The pet you've been hiding since our camping trip."

She crossed the room to stand protectively in front of her dresser. "I'm not hiding anything in my drawer. I haven't even seen a fuzzy pet. So go away."

I almost laughed, she was such a bad liar.

But before I could say anything, a skinny creature wiggled out of a drawer. It reminded me of a furry Slinky, with no arms or legs, and only a round head bobbing on a shaggy snake body. I shivered when it coiled into the air and blinked a large purple eye at me.

"The goofink!" I grabbed my sister. "Get away from it, Amber! It could be dangerous."

"It's not an *it*, she's a girl." Amber pulled away from me and scooped the furry pet to her chest. "Her name is Jennifer."

The goofink—Jennifer—purred as she rubbed her fuzzy head against my sister. The purple eye closed contentedly. And the purring grew louder, a sweet symphony spilling out of the slinky furball.

"Her music is amazing!" I said in astonishment.

"Jennifer sounds pretty. You can pet her—she won't hurt you."

Timidly, I reached out. Touching the strange creature was like sinking my fingers into silky clouds. The purring vibrated through me, making me feel happy.

"I told you Jennifer was nice," Amber said.

"Yeah, but you can't keep her. She's not from here." I pulled my hand back. "Amber, haven't you noticed anything different about her?"

"Well . . . maybe. She knocks stuff over when she dances."

"How can she dance without legs?"

"She sways on her tail. She likes jazz best. She likes me, too, and is really nice even when she—" Amber hesitated, touching the scratch on her chin.

"Did she attack you?" I demanded.

"She didn't mean to. It was 'cause she was hungry."

"She tried to eat you!"

"No, silly. Jennifer is picky. She won't even drink water. But she loves my hair."

"Your hair!" Horrified, I looked closely at Amber. Her golden hair had ragged edges and was missing curls.

"It doesn't hurt," my sister insisted. "It tickles."

"Amber, this has to stop. Or you'll be bald by the time school starts."

"Bald?" Her blue eyes welled up with tears. "But I don't wanna be bald."

"Then get rid of Jennifer."

"But I love her."

"More than you love your hair?" I challenged.

"I—I don't know."

"You can't keep her."

"She doesn't have any family. She needs me."

"And you need your hair. Give her to me."

"Only if you take care of her and make sure no one hurts her."

"Okay."

"Double pinky promise?"

I held up both pinky fingers and crossed them. "I promise."

Amber sniffled and hugged Jennifer. Then she handed me the goofink. "You win, Cassie," she said sadly.

Only I didn't feel like I'd won. Instead, I felt scared and worried. What in the world was I going to do with an alien pet?

And how could I stop her from eating *my* hair?

chapter thirteen
Shasta
Secrets

I sent Amber off to lunch and then took Jennifer into my room.

"You'll be safe here," I said, placing her in a dresser drawer.

She blinked her big eye once as if nodding okay.

"No dancing or messing things up while I'm gone." I walked over to my suitcase and pulled out my brush. I plucked a few hairs from the bristles. "Be good and I'll give you more when I come back."

Jennifer slurped the hairs, then blinked twice as if saying thank you. At least, that's what I hoped she was saying. It could have been, "That was a good snack, where's lunch?"

I held onto my hair protectively as I hurried out of the room.

As I headed back to my parents' room, I thought about Hank. Where had he gone so abruptly? Was it because of Trevor? The pint-sized actor was annoying, but that was no reason for Hank to leave. So why had he rushed off?

The easiest way to find out was to ask Hank. So instead of going to my parents' room, I went to the suite next door.

Only it wasn't Hank who answered my knock.

"Trevor!" I exclaimed. "What are you doing in Hank's room?"

Trevor raised his eyebrows. "This is *my* room."

"But he told me—You have to know him—" I rubbed my forehead.

Lucas came up beside the smaller boy. "Cassie, what's up?"

"That's what I want to find out. I thought this was Hank's room."

"So did I." My brother shrugged. "But it's not."

"Who's Hank?" Trevor asked.

"A kid with a great throwing arm," Lucas said, grinning. "You'd like him."

"I doubt that." Trevor tugged on Lucas's arm. "Come on, let's finish running lines." Then he slammed the door in my face.

Why that rude jerk! I fumed. I'd like to slam something in his face!

Was Lucas so blinded by Hollywood stars that he couldn't see what an obnoxious creep Trevor was? Maybe Hank could help me talk some sense into my brother. It was worth a try anyway. So I went to the resort office to find out Hank's room number.

A shaggy-haired, burly elderly man sat at the front desk, flipping through a newspaper. He didn't notice me, so I pressed a buzzer on the counter.

A loud *Phzzzt* erupted, and he jumped out of his chair, his paper falling to the floor. He picked it up, then smiled at me. "Good afternoon. You must be the young lady my wife told me about. Cathy, right?"

"Cassie," I corrected. "Sorry I startled you."

"That's all right. I was just reading the latest about our leprechaun. He's becoming big news around here. And now your father's going to put him on TV."

"You really saw a leprechaun?"

"Sure did. A little redhead about so high." He held out his hand level with my shoulders. "Wearing all green except for pointy gold slippers. I would have caught him if I hadn't fallen into a hole covered by brush."

"A booby trap?"

He nodded. "Lucky I didn't break my leg."

"Maybe it's a kid dressed like a leprechaun," I said.

"Can a kid summon a rainbow, then fly away on it? And how do you explain a pool swarming with catfish?" The elderly man shook his head. "It's magic."

"Wow" was all I could say. It would be so cool to see the leprechaun—maybe hop a ride on his rainbow and find his pot of gold. Then I'd be rich enough to join Club Glorious and hang out with Rosalie and her Glorious friends. But I reminded myself why my family was here. Leprechauns were NOT real—and Dad would prove it.

"Was there something I could do for you?" Mr. Truelock asked.

"I'm looking for a friend who's staying here. I don't know his last name, but his first name is Hank."

"Only three kids registered—you, your brother, and the Tremaine boy."

"But I saw Hank just a while ago. His family has one of the suites."

"Sorry. Never heard of him." Then he barked out a laugh. "Maybe he's staying with the leprechaun."

Mr. Truelock was still laughing as I stomped out of the room.

• • •

An hour later, Amber and I were relaxing on my parents' luxurious king-size bed, snacking on wheat-germ chips while we watched a movie on the big-screen TV, when Dad announced he was driving into Mount Shasta.

"Want to come along?" he invited. "You girls can enjoy the shops while I interview a few people."

He didn't need to ask me twice. Before we left, I went to check on the goofink.

When I opened my door, it looked like a tornado had swept through the room. Blankets, clothes, pillows, books, and shoes were scattered everywhere.

Hurricane Jennifer was curled on the bed, nibbling on my hairbrush.

"Jennifer!" I wagged my finger at her. "I told you not to dance in here."

She bounced into my arms and purred against me.

"You're a bad girl," I told her.

Her purring was a sweet, soothing chorus, and my anger changed to happiness. She really was cute, and holding her felt nice. I had no idea what I was going to do with her, but I'd figure that out later. I offered Jennifer a few strands of my hair, then tucked her in the drawer and promised to return in a few hours.

I hoped I wasn't making a mistake leaving her behind.

The ride into the town of Mount Shasta took about fifteen minutes. I enjoyed having the middle seat to myself since Lucas had stayed behind with Trevor. Mom told us the snow-topped mountain in the distance was Mount Shasta and that it was over 14,000 feet high.

"The brochure says it's one of the Seven Sacred Mountains of the world," Mom added. "The name 'Shasta' came from a Russian word meaning 'good luck.' And the volcanic mountain draws people from around the world. It's considered sacred and magical."

Magical? I wondered. As in little green lep-rechauns?

We pulled into town, and Dad left for his interview, so Mom, Amber, and I checked out the shops. Amber found a floppy stuffed monkey in a store that sold greeting cards and toys. Mom couldn't resist a store offering holistic remedies. I wasn't sure what "holistic" meant, but it must be something healthy since Mom liked it.

Then Mom took us into a store called The Crystal Room. At first I thought a bunch of rocks would be boring. But when we went into a special back room, I couldn't believe the size of this huge cluster of quartz on display. It was as tall as my bicycle and as wide as a couch. Most stores warned kids not to touch things, but a friendly clerk encouraged us to run our fingers all over the quartz. It felt smooth and cool. Mom was pleased with our interest and let us each pick out a tiny animal-shaped rock as a souvenir. Amber chose a jade frog, and I picked a rose quartz cat. The clerk said they'd bring us good luck and gave us cloth pouches to carry them in.

Moments later, my pouch was tucked in my pocket as we entered a bookstore. Mom went straight to the herb section while Amber plopped in a kiddie chair to read a picture book called *The Inside Tree*. I wandered over to a display of books on Mount Shasta.

A large spiral-bound book caught my eye: *Mountain Mysteries and Lore*. I skimmed through the table of contents. History, geography, and photos of tourist sites didn't interest me. But my heart quickened when I found a chapter entitled "Big Secrets about Little People."

The story made me think of tall tales whispered on dark, stormy nights. A lost civilization of mystical people who could fly, talk without speaking aloud, and teleport using mind power. They existed in harmony with nature—until a terrible flood destroyed their city. Survivors moved into secret tunnels under Mount Shasta.

It was only a legend, the author of the article explained. But many people reported seeing strange lights and unusual sounds around Mount Shasta.

One person even claimed to have a picture of a magical little person.

I turned the page to see this picture—and gasped.

It was Hank.

chapter fourteen

Magic and Mischief

When we returned to the resort, I searched everywhere for Hank, but no one had seen him or had any idea where he lived.

It was as if he never existed.

He's not a leprechaun, I told myself over and over, hoping to convince myself. I longed to talk this over with Lucas, but he was still off with Trevor.

Discouraged, I headed for the barn. I was glad to find Jennifer asleep in her drawer. Careful not to wake her, I reached under my bed for Grandma's box.

I opened it and pulled out my journal. The words "KEEP OUT! DEATH TO ANYONE SNOOPING" blazed in bold black across the cover.

It's me again, I wrote. *And boy am I confused!*

Meeting Vee taught me that unusual things do happen, but it's hard to know what to believe. Dad is so sure that everything has a logical explanation. He can always find some way to prove what he thinks is true. But my problems aren't that easy to explain. I mean, how can I explain Hank?

He said he was a resort guest, but he isn't registered.

He disappeared so suddenly—like magic.

The picture in the book looked like him.

And how did he get up in that tree?

I closed my journal and frowned. There was one logical explanation, but it defied everything logical. Hank couldn't be a leprechaun. He didn't wear green or look magical. He was just a regular kid, like me. But I couldn't stop thinking about the golden-eyed boy in the picture. The only way to know for sure was to ask Hank for the truth.

But first I had to find him. And I'd start looking first thing in the . . .

• • •

The next morning, I woke up to screaming.

That sounds like Mrs. Truelock, I thought as I tossed aside my covers and jumped out of bed. Slipping on my robe, I looked around for my slippers but couldn't find them. So I ran outside barefoot.

An excited group of people gathered in the front of the main building. Mom, Dad, a mustached man who resembled Trevor, and the Truelocks. All of them were pointing up at something.

Following their gazes, I stared in astonishment at an oak tree.

Mom was always teaching me about nature, so I knew this was a very old tree by its thick trunk. The majestic oak had stood proud and tall in this spot long before the resort was built. But all pride was gone today.

Shoes dangled down from dozens of branches. Sneakers, boots, sandals, dress shoes, high heels, and even a familiar blue fluffy slipper.

"That's my slipper!" I exclaimed. "But how did it get up there?"

"That's what we're all wondering, Cassie," Mom said, glancing down at her own socked feet. That's when I noticed everyone was either barefoot or wearing socks.

"This is an outrage," the man with the mustache complained with the same arrogant tone Trevor used before slamming the door in my face. "What kind of resort allows a thief to sneak into our private rooms and steal our belongings?"

"I assure you, Mr. Tremaine," Mr. Truelock said, clearing his throat. "Your shoes will be returned."

"Just how are you going to accomplish that? You don't look like you're in any shape to climb a tree."

"You want to climb it?" Mr. Truelock retorted. "Like to see you try in those sissy pink socks."

Trevor's father made a humph sound, then spun around on his stocking feet and strode back into the building.

I glanced over at Mrs. Truelock, who looked close to tears. "The prankster is ruining everything."

"Our shoes aren't ruined, they're just tied up," I tried to reassure her.

"Way up," Lucas added.

"But my resort is falling apart. Most of our rooms can't be used; the pool is filled with fish; and there's a bird sitting on my silver sandal." She buried her face in her husband's shoulder.

"Don't you worry, Sugarkins." Mr. Truelock patted her shoulder. "I'll take care of things."

"Find a ladder, and I'll climb the tree," my father offered. "I may even get fingerprints off the shoes. We'll find that prankster before he can cause more trouble."

"Fingerprints won't stop a leprechaun," Mr. Truelock said. "Don't you know anything about magical beings? We'll have to find his pot of gold and force him to grant us wishes."

"Really, Truelock," my father said with an impatient tap of his white-socked foot. "You don't believe that nonsense?"

"I most certainly do. And you would, too, if you saw what I did."

"Leprechauns are a myth. Someone is pulling your leg, and I'll prove it."

"Just stop the pranks," Mrs. Truelock sobbed. "I can't take any more."

I felt sorry for the Truelocks and angry at Hank. Leprechaun or not, I knew he was behind these pranks. And I was determined to make him stop. But I couldn't search the woods wearing only socks, so I returned to the barn.

As I neared my room, I heard music. Oh, no! I thought in dismay. Jennifer is at it again!

And when I opened the door, there was Jennifer, bouncing on her tail like a fuzzy pogo stick—only she wasn't dancing alone.

She was hip-hopping with Hank!

Jennifer blinked guiltily at me. The music stopped, and she hid behind Hank.

"Neato mosquito!" Hank grinned. "I've always wanted to dance with a goofink."

"You *know* about goofinks?" I asked in astonishment.

"Sure. But they're so rare, I've only seen them in books."

"I saw something amazing in a book yesterday," I murmured, my legs feeling wobbly. "I didn't think it was true—didn't want to believe it. But it is, isn't it?"

"What book?"

"Mountain Mysteries and Lore."

"Oh." Hank bit his lip. "You saw the picture?"

I nodded.

Hank stepped away from Jennifer and gave me a wary look. It was the first time I'd seen him without a smile, and I felt uneasy. If he was magical, what powers did he have? And how could I stop him from using them on me?

"You—you really are a leprechaun?" I asked nervously.

"No."

"Thank goodness." I sank into a chair in relief. "For a minute there, I was really freaking out. I mean, magic isn't real. That's what my parents have always told—"

"But I am related to leprechauns," he interrupted. "Distant cousins."

"Oh." I sighed. "So you are magic?"

"If you want to call it magic." His ever-changing eyes twinkled. "But my people explain our abilities with science. To me, flying is as ordinary as walking is to you."

"You can fly?"

"Better than a bird. And I can vanish and other tricks."

"The green slime, catfish, and booby traps." I pointed at him accusingly. "Why did you do them?"

"For laughs. Everyone is so serious where I'm from, so I ran away to have fun."

"Ran away from where?"

"Under the mountain. The passages are secret, and it's forbidden to have contact with outsiders."

"So you came here to hurt innocent people?"

"I didn't hurt anyone."

"Yes, you did," I argued. "Mrs. Truelock was crying. She's miserable because you're ruining her business with all your dumb pranks."

"What do you mean 'dumb'? That shoe tree was my best trick yet. And wait till you see what I have planned for tomorrow."

I wagged my finger at him. "You will NOT do anything else. No more slime or fish or shoes! Or I'll—I'll—"

"What?" He chuckled. "Turn me into a toad? Last time I checked, I was the one with magic. Not you."

"This is not funny! You have to stop."

"Okay." He folded his legs and floated up to the ceiling.

My mouth fell open, and I just stared. Suspecting he was magical was one thing, but seeing it up close was scary. I backed off, reaching behind me for the door. I was ready to run until I realized what he'd just said.

"You really will stop?" I asked in a small voice.

"On one condition."

I didn't like the wicked arch of his eyebrows. "What?" I asked.

"That you play a game with me. If you win, I'll return home and stop the pranks."

"How can I trust you?"

"Once I make a promise, I am honor bound to keep it."

I couldn't see the harm in just one game, especially if I could help Mrs. Truelock. "Okay. It's a deal."

"And the game starts now." His eyes flashed gold and there was a sizzling *CRAAACK!* sound. Then he was gone and a paper curled in my hand.

I unfolded it and found myself staring at a treasure map.

chapter fifteen

Booby
Trapped

This map wasn't like the one Lucas had made. It crinkled with authenticity—spidery black ink on fine yellow-gold paper. There were no words, only cryptic markings within an unmistakable outline of Mount Shasta. Wavy lines were either rivers or roads. And tiny shapes offered clues: a rabbit, a fork, a black cat, and a yellow shamrock.

"Not yellow," I murmured. "But gold—a golden shamrock!"

I jumped excitedly. Now I knew where to start. And the wavy black X high within the craggy outline of Mount Shasta showed my destination. X marks the spot, right? But how would I get there?

The answer came that evening when Mom told me to get plenty of sleep because in the morning we were going hiking on Mount Shasta trails. Normally, I groaned at exercise, but according to the map, the path to the "treasure" started near the 8,000-foot elevation.

I was tempted to invite Lucas to join my game— until I remembered his smug attitude when I couldn't figure out his lame map. Besides, he ditched me to spend the whole day with Trevor. If he'd rather be with that stuck-up kid actor, that was fine with me. I didn't need his help.

I'll show you, Lucas, I thought. I'll find a real treasure all by myself.

• • •

As I tucked Jennifer into her drawer that evening, I heard shouting. Grabbing a jacket and slipping on my shoes, I hurried outside.

A red-gold sunset cast an eerie glow as day sunk into twilight. I saw Lucas running and heard another distant shout.

"That's Dad," Lucas called out.

"Sounds like he's in trouble!"

"Come on!" Lucas sprinted past me. "Run faster."

"I'm trying—oops!" I stumbled over a dirt clod.

Weeds crunched under my sneakers, and branches snagged my clothes and hair. Dad's frantic shouts grew louder. Was a wild animal attacking him?

My brother disappeared over a small hill. As I neared the top of the hill, I heard him holler, "Found him!" But when I reached Lucas, there was no sign of Dad.

I looked around, puzzled. "Where is he?" I asked.

"Up here," Dad answered.

I looked up and saw my dignified father dangling upside down from a tree, like a human piñata.

"Get me down!" he roared.

"How?" I asked.

"I don't care!" His face puffed red. "Just do it!"

"But there aren't any low branches," Lucas pointed out. "There's no way to climb up there."

"Find a ladder before my head explodes!"

"Okay." Lucas spun around and started back.

I caught his sleeve. "Wait. It'll take too long to find a ladder tall enough." I studied how the rope around Dad's ankles trailed down a branch, snaked through two trees, and then looped around a large volcanic rock. "I think I know a better way."

"What?" Lucas asked.

"If we untie the other end of the rope, we can use our weight to balance Dad and then lower him slowly to the ground."

"That's called leverage. I learned about it in advanced science," Lucas said. "And I know how to untie tough knots. Stand back while I work my magic."

I stood back, but Lucas's "magic" turned out to be rusty. He tugged and twisted, groaned and griped. Finally, he sliced the rope with his pocketknife.

"Told you I was good with ropes," he said.

Heaving and pulling, we managed to lower Dad gently to the ground. He tried to stand, but his legs crumpled, and he gave an exhausted cry. He would have tumbled to the ground if we hadn't propped him up on our shoulders.

"Everything is spinning," Dad murmured.

"You want to sit down?" I asked.

"No. I'll be okay." He smiled feebly at us. "Thanks, kids."

"How'd you get up there?" Lucas asked.

"I'm not sure. I heard laughter and came out here to investigate." Dad rubbed his reddened face. "Suddenly, a rope yanked me off the ground, and I found myself swinging upside down in the air."

"A booby trap." Lucas snapped his fingers.

"Yeah. But while I was hanging there, I saw something odd . . ." Dad scratched his chin as his words trailed off. "I'm sure I imagined it."

"Imagined what?" I asked.

"A little red-haired guy wearing a shiny green suit."

"A leprechaun!" Lucas said.

"They don't exist. It's probably a kid playing tricks. Although I can't figure out how he . . ." Dad stared up, his voice trailing off again.

"What?" both Lucas and I asked.

"Flew to the tree top—then vanished."

"Like magic!" I exclaimed.

"Impossible," Dad insisted firmly. "I've investigated hundreds of unusual happenings, and I've always found a logical explanation. Someone went to a lot of trouble to fool me. And you know what that means."

Lucas and I shook our heads.

"War." Dad's gray eyes narrowed.

I gulped. "What are you doing to do?"

"Bring in my TV crew to search every inch of these woods until we find the prankster. I'll prove he's a fake and make sure he never bothers anyone again."

"How?" I asked nervously.

"I'll have him arrested. The little green guy is going to jail."

chapter sixteen

The Game
Begins

I'd never seen Dad so angry. Not even magical
powers could help Hank if Dad caught up with him.
Someone had to warn him.

But I had no way of finding him—except the
map. Also, Dad's description of the prankster confused me. Hank's hair was brown, not red. And I'd
never seen him wear shiny green clothes. Was that
a disguise or the real Hank?

While the goofink purred a tune from the drawer, I
studied the map. I recognized the high peak of Mount

Shasta, but couldn't figure out the squiggly lines. And what did the cat, rabbit, and fork mean?

When I finally fell asleep, I tossed with nightmares. Dad dragged Hank out of a tree and ripped off his golden wings so he couldn't fly. Hank was bound in chains, then thrown into an awful dark dungeon. Powerless, Hank rattled the bars, making a horrible noise that hurt my ears.

Not prison bars, I realized as I awoke. My buzzing alarm clock.

And I was late!

By the time I made it to my parents' suite, everyone had finished breakfast. I had decided to tell Lucas about Hank, but there wasn't a chance. I gulped down some berry juice, grabbed a cinnamon rice cake, and then hurried to the van.

Dad had fully recovered from his piñata experience. He sang cheerfully to his favorite country music CD. If Dad was happy, that meant trouble for Hank. I had to warn him before Dad's TV crew arrived.

Mom read from a brochure as Dad drove. "It's a beautiful drive up the Everitt Memorial Highway into Mount Shasta wilderness."

"Will I see any bears?" Lucas asked, pressing close to a window.

"Not likely," Dad said. "Bears tend to stay away from humans."

"Watch the woods for movement, though," Mom added, "you might see a deer."

"Deer are boring," Lucas complained. But he turned back to the window, and it wasn't long before he spotted a doe and her fawn leaping up a hillside.

The mention of wild bears gave me shivers. I hoped Dad was right about bears avoiding humans—because I definitely wanted to avoid bears.

We climbed higher and higher up the road. Lucas had switched from watching out the window to listening to his headphones, and Amber was so silent I guessed she was asleep. But when I turned around to check, I had a déjà-vu shock.

Curled on my sister's lap was the goofink.

"Amber!" I whispered angrily. "How could you bring her?"

"It was easy."

"You snuck into my room!"

"Shush." Amber put her finger to her lips. "Jennifer's sleeping."

I wanted to forget all about the goofink. But what if the hair-eating creature attacked Amber? Or, worse, what if Mom and Dad saw it, freaked, and we didn't go on our hike? I'd never find Hank! So I bluffed and threatened to tell Mom and Dad if Amber didn't give Jennifer to me. With a sniffle, she handed Jennifer over.

When I tucked the goofink under my shirt, its silky fur tickled, and I giggled.

"Did you say something?" Lucas lifted his headphones and turned toward me.

"Just talking to myself."

He shrugged and turned away.

A short time later, we reached our first stop.

"Everyone out for Bunny Flat," Mom announced. "There's a scenic trail for hiking."

Lucas eyed the ice chest Mom had packed. "I'd rather eat lunch."

"Not till our next stop. Panther Meadows has picnic tables."

"Panther Meadows?" I asked with interest. "And this is called Bunny Flat?"

Mom nodded. "The brochure says we'll see plenty of wild plants."

And leprechauns? I wondered, guessing the rabbit and cat drawn on the map represented Bunny Flat and Panther Meadows.

● ● ●

The hike was fun—except for Jennifer. She kept tickling me under my T-shirt. I'd huff and puff up a hill, then start giggling. Everyone looked at me weird—except Amber, who giggled too. When I returned to the van, I switched Jennifer's hiding place to my backpack. It also contained water bottles, granola bars, a flashlight, and a compass. I was prepared for anything—I hoped.

There were only a few cars in the Panther Meadows parking lot. Mom snagged an empty picnic table, and while my family set out the food, I pretended to trip on a rock, stumbling forward on my hands—directly into a mud puddle.

Dad scooted over and helped me up. "You okay, Cassie?"

"Yeah. But I'm all dirty." I held out my palms. "I better wash up."

"There isn't a water faucet here," Mom pointed out.

I'd expected that and was ready with my answer. "I'll use the natural spring I read about in a brochure. It's supposed to be a sacred place, and I wanted to see it anyway. It's just over that hill."

Mom smiled. "I'm happy to see you showing an interest in nature. When you get back, I can show you a petition I'm starting to save the—"

"I better hurry," I interrupted before Mom launched into a boring lecture. "I won't be long."

Then I grabbed my backpack and trudged up a hilly path.

Once I was alone (except for Jennifer), I studied the map. A squiggly line connected the bunny to the panther. Then the line continued up, crossing more squiggles and making a windy path from the panther almost to the X mark. Then the path branched out into a tiny upside-down Y. Or maybe it was a broom. I'd have to figure that out to reach the black X mark. Then what would happen?

There was only one way to find out.

The game had begun!

As I started on the trail, I tensed at every small sound. And I wondered why it was called Panther Meadows. Luckily, the only wild animal I saw was a squirrel—and he seemed more scared of me.

I wound through a cluster of trees until I came to a lush green meadow. Tall grass swished against my legs. When the trail branched off, I stopped to check the map. Then I veered left until I reached a spring spilling down a hillside. This matched a wavy mark on the map.

My backpack dug into my shoulders, so I slipped it off. Then I knelt down and rubbed my hands together in the icy water. Dirt washed away, and my hands tingled from the chill. Straightening, I dried my hands on my jeans, feeling the bump of the quartz cat in my pocket. I hoped it would give me good luck.

Then I lifted up the map again and was studying it when I heard a footstep crunch behind me.

I whirled around. "What are you doing here?"

My brother grabbed my arm. "Hide me!"

"From what?"

"Trevor." Lucas looked over his shoulder. "He's stalking me."

Even though Lucas was messing up my plans, I couldn't resist a grin. Obviously things weren't going well in movie-star land.

"I thought I'd ditched him, but he just showed up with his father."

"So he's going hiking." I shrugged. "Big deal."

"No! He won't leave me alone."

"I thought you *admired* him."

"No one admires Trevor as much as he admires himself. He keeps bragging about his roles and showing off his dumb photo albums. And if I hear his Chuckle-Cookie laugh one more time, I'll barf."

"Well, you can't stay with me."

"Why not?" Lucas narrowed his gaze. "What are you really doing here? And what's that paper you're holding? It looks like a—"

"Nothing!" I cut him off and swung my hand behind my back. "Aren't you missing lunch? Mom packed your favorite wheat-germ chips."

"It's a map, isn't it?"

"And there's pineapple-cranberry juice. Hurry back," I said in my best sweet, older-sister voice.

"Show me the map, Cassie."

"NO!"

"Who gave it to you?"

"It doesn't matter."

"Who?" Lucas persisted.

"Hank. Now go play with Trevor and leave me alone."

But as I jerked away, he lunged for the paper.

And the map ripped in two.

"You ruined it!" I cried, waving my jagged half.

"I didn't mean . . ." His words trailed off, and he stared ahead with a shocked expression. He wasn't even looking at the torn map. His hand shook as pointed to my backpack, where a furry alien head poked out. "What—what is it?"

"Lucas," I said after a long pause, "meet Jennifer."

chapter seventeen

Bridge to Magic

"But what *is* she?" My brother stared in astonishment. "And where did she come from?"

"I'll tell you, if you give me the rest of my map."

"Okay." He quickly handed over the paper and backed away from Jennifer.

"But you can't tell anyone. This is top secret."

He nodded solemnly.

"It started on our camping trip," I began. Then I explained about the banana-shaped spaceship, my alien friend Vee, and the dancing goofink.

"Wow" was all he said when I finished.

"Do you believe me?"

"How can I argue when I'm staring at that thing?" Lucas regarded Jennifer nervously. "Will she bite?"

"Only your hair. She's friendly. Go ahead, pet her."

"I—I don't . . . Okay." He hesitated, then reached out his hand. "She's purring. I think she likes me."

"She's really sweet. But she doesn't belong on this planet, and I have no idea what to do with her." I sighed. "I'll figure that out later. Now it's more urgent to warn Hank about Dad."

"I'll help," Lucas offered.

"You just want to find a treasure."

"So do you," he teased. And I couldn't argue.

We set off on a trail over a rocky hill. Lucas held the map halves, and Jennifer slept contentedly on my shoulders in the backpack. I figured we had at least twenty minutes before Mom and Dad came looking for us. We had to find Hank fast.

"Does that burned tree look like a fork?" Lucas pointed.

"No," I said with a shake of my head. "What about that twisted bush?"

"Not even close."

So we kept going. We crossed a log propped over a small stream, scaled a narrow rock plateau, and pushed through a maze of high weeds. We walked and walked, higher and higher, but nothing resembled a fork.

Lucas groaned. "This is hopeless."

"The map shows the trail branching off that way," I said, gesturing to the right.

"Are you sure it's a trail? I only see trees. We should go back."

I remembered how bad I felt when I gave up on his map—like a failure. "No." I shook my head. "I'm not quitting."

"You'd rather get lost?"

"You'd rather go back to Trevor?"

Lucas made a bitter face. "Why are we standing around? Let's find Hank's treasure."

I hid my smile as we trudged on again.

A short while later, the trail ended at a waterfall. To the right was a sharp cliff and to the left a wall of thorny bushes.

"A dead end," Lucas said, sounding a bit relieved. "Now we'll have to give up."

"No!" I stomped my foot. "That fork has to be here somewhere."

"Unless Hank is playing another prank."

"I don't think so." I pointed at the map. "The wavy lines are the waterfall, and the dark area is the cliff. So the fork should be there."

"Over the cliff?" he scoffed. "Not unless forks can fly."

"I know it doesn't make sense. Maybe these marks are a clue."

Lucas peered at tiny twin circles. "Looks like footprints."

"Footprints?" I wrinkled my brow. "Hey, you might be right. Maybe it's telling us where to put our feet."

"Over here," Lucas said, stopping directly in front of the waterfall.

We stood side by side before a sharp drop-off that seemed to plunge down for miles. Foamy spray splashed my face, and I squinted through bright rays of sunshine. Rushing water drowned out everything except the pounding of my heart. Chilly air cut through my clothes.

When I heard the music, I thought it was Jennifer. But the melody came from within the waterfall. I stared in astonishment as a dome formed inside the cascading water. A teardrop dangled from the ceiling of the dome and a spire rose at the top into a rounded peak. The teardrop swayed and chimes rang out.

Not a fork, I realized with excitement. It's a giant bell!

Water rushed around the dome but not inside. The tonguelike ringer stretched longer and longer until it became a translucent bridge that crossed the chasm between the waterfall and our side of the cliff.

A secret tunnel into Mount Shasta!

"The legend is true!" I clutched my brother's hand, both afraid and thrilled. "We've found the entrance."

"Into what?" he asked in a hushed voice.

"A hidden community of magical people—Hank's people."

We stood there, spellbound, as the silvery bridge spanned over glistening water, reaching out to us. We looked at each other, hesitating.

"Are we . . . going in?" Lucas asked.

"I think I have to."

"Then me too."

We stepped cautiously onto the bridge. Water rained down on each side, yet not a drop touched us. Foam churned over jutted rocks below, so very far down that I felt dizzy. I forced myself to look ahead, to keep going.

Then we were inside a cavern darker than nightmares.

Whoosh! Behind us, the silvery bridge curled up and the cloudlike bell faded to mist. The waterfall flowed again. Only, now Lucas and I watched it from inside the mountain.

"Neato mosquito!" a laughing voice rang out. And there was Hank, wearing his leather jacket and cowboy boots, looking nothing like a magical being.

"What is this place?" I asked in awe.

"My home." He pointed at the cave opening and there was a bright flash. "Congratulations on a game well played. You win."

Then the cave closed up—trapping us inside.

chapter eighteen

True Stories

I tried not to panic—and failed miserably.

"Let us out!" I pounded on the closed wall. "You can't keep us prisoners."

"You're not prisoners." Hank smiled. "You're my friends."

"Then show us the way out," Lucas asked.

"Not until I show you around. You're gonna love this! Come on."

What sort of game is he playing? I wondered. With the cave entrance closed, there was only one way to go. So we followed Hank deeper into the tunnel.

The sound of rushing water faded as we entered an arched passage lit by brilliant flickering bulbs. I looked closer and realized they weren't lightbulbs, but tiny electric creatures—like the fireflies I'd seen when I'd visited Aunt Betty Jo in Indiana.

Our footsteps were silent—as if we walked on cotton. Dark rock walls brightened to clear crystal and I could see my own reflection moving beside me. My gray eyes were wide, and my cheeks flushed with excitement—like when I forced myself to ride the Death Spiral at the Thrill Land.

"That's the Celestial Chamber," Hank said as we passed a star-shaped door. "Only the ancient ones are allowed."

"What do they do in there?" I asked.

"Communicate with distant friends."

"In other countries—like Europe and Australia?" Lucas guessed.

"More distant." Hank pointed up. "Beyond the stars and planets. But I can't say any more. There are some rules even I won't break."

He led us around a corner where the passage narrowed. I noticed a small brick door almost hidden in the wall. "What's in there?"

"Nothing interesting—just diamonds, rubies, and emeralds."

"Nothing interesting?! But jewels are worth lots of money. One tiny little diamond would buy a hundred memberships at Club Glorious," I added wistfully.

"Money has no value here. I'll show you something better." Hank gestured toward a doorway embedded with round blue, red, and green buttons. He touched a green button and his finger glowed. Instead of the door swinging in or out, it simply vanished. And we stepped inside.

The domed room was empty except for shadows flickering across walls. Bright lights fluttered in the ceiling and soft murmurs swirled around us.

"This is the Story Chamber," Hank told us.

"What are those sounds?" I asked.

"Whispers. They're waiting for you."

"Who?" Lucas asked uneasily.

"Memory folk." Hank walked over to a wall and pointed to the shadows. "Each has millions of stories to tell. All you have to do is ask."

"What kind of stories?"

"Real ones."

"A history lesson," I said, disappointed. "I get enough of that in school."

"I'd rather hear something exciting, like *The Three Musketeers* or *A Midsummer Night's Dream*," Lucas said.

"Or the *Lord of the Rings*," I added with a meaningful look at Hank. He was short enough to be a hobbit and his home reminded me of Middle Earth.

"But those stories *are* real," Hank insisted.

"No way," Lucas scoffed.

"Imagination is truth in disguise. Where do you think Tolkien and Shakespeare got their ideas?" Chuckling, Hank urged us to try a story.

My eyes adjusted to the shadow's quicksilver movement, and I made out the gentle face of a woman. Long sleeves rustled as she reached out and whispered, "Ask, ask, ask."

"Well . . . okay." I swallowed hard. "Could you please tell me a story?"

A strong breeze swept over me. Alphabet letters flitted in the air like tiny birds. I felt loving arms hold me snugly on a warm lap. The woman's beautiful voice kept me spellbound as she began her story.

"There was a young girl named Kathy who looked very much like you. She loved flowers, trees, and wild animals. Her long brown braid danced in the wind as she played in the woods. She would sit on wild grass under shady branches for hours, drawing pictures."

The storyteller drew me into Kathy's world. Sitting beside her, I watched her draw a puffy-cheeked squirrel and a wide-eyed fawn. I smelled pine, heard birds, and felt the cooling kiss of summer breezes.

"But alas, Kathy's family owned a construction business that planned to cut down the woods to make new homes for families," the storyteller continued.

"No!" I gasped.

"This made Kathy very sad. 'What about the families already living in the woods?' Kathy cried. 'The birds, deer, squirrels, and other animals? Please don't destroy their homes.' But Kathy's parents refused and told her, 'You're too little to understand.'

"Kathy was little on the outside, but she was big inside. She started a petition to save the woods. She gathered hundreds of signatures and took them to the mayor. That didn't work, but the petition caught the attention of a local TV station. She was invited on TV to tell people about the woods. She showed her drawings of stately trees and wondrous creatures. A wealthy woman was watching and offered to help. She bought the woods, and donated them to the city in Kathy's name. The forest became a wildlife sanctuary that will be protected forever."

"What about Kathy?" I asked. "What happened to her?"

"Why, she grew up of course! She married a news reporter from the TV station, and she named her first daughter Cassandra." The storyteller whispered "Farewell," then disappeared into the crystal wall.

I stared with astonishment. *My* name was Cassandra! Mom's name was Katherine, and Dad used to be a news reporter. Maybe Mom's petitions weren't so dumb after all. Each one was like a helping hand to the world. People like Mom made things happen.

Lucas came up beside me. "I heard the best story! About a reporter who pretends to be a rich, old lady to expose a jewel thief. Boy was that thief surprised when the guy ripped off his mask and knocked him to the ground. It felt so real, like it really happened."

"Maybe it did," I told him.

Then we followed Hank out of the room.

We only walked a short distance before he pointed at a pale blue, oval-shaped door.

"This is the Healing Chamber," Hank said, the doorway vanishing at his touch.

Peering inside, I saw a huge room filled with crystal bowls of all sizes, tiny as a fist to one as large as a refrigerator. A few of the bowls were spinning and humming with energy.

"Why are there so many bowls?" I asked.

"To treat many ailments. They heal with sound vibrations."

"Cool," Lucas said. "Show us how they work."

Hank shook his head. "This room is sacred. If the elders knew you were here, they'd throw us all in the Pit."

"The Pit?" I gulped. "What's that?"

"You don't want to find out. But you're safe because no one knows you're—" Hank stopped. "Someone's coming!"

"Oh, no!" I looked around in panic. "What should we do?"

"Hurry—*hide!*"

"Where?" Lucas and I asked.

"Inside there." Hank pointed to the largest crystal bowl.

chapter nineteen

Imagine
Nation

Lucas and I ducked into the bowl.

"You can see out, but no one can see in," Hank
explained.

"Like a two-way mirror," I murmured.

"It would be great for hide 'n' seek," Lucas said.

The bowl didn't move, yet it seemed to vibrate and
tingle—like a shower of sunshine. I relaxed and
stopped feeling afraid. I could tell Jennifer liked the
bowl, too, because the purring in my backpack grew
louder.

A very tall, very thin man in a yellow robe came up to Hank. "Greetings, Master Ventoya," Hank said respectfully.

"Greetings, young Hanniscorn." The man's stern, jagged faced reminded me of a bronze sculpture. "What brings you so far from your private chamber?"

"My rhythms were slow, so I sought out healing sound."

"I trust you are well now?"

"Very well," Hank replied formally. "Thank you for your concern."

"Welcome returned." He gave a deep bow. "I bid you a good day." Then he moved on down the corridor.

"It's safe," Hank called. "Come on out."

Refreshed as if I'd awoken from a peaceful sleep, I followed Lucas out of the bell.

"What did that tall dude call you?" Lucas asked.

"Hanniscorn is my formal name, but I prefer Hank. Master Ventoya is an important seventh-level elder."

"Seventh level?" I wrinkled my brow. "So he's like seventy years old?"

Hank slapped his knee and laughed. "Good one, Cassie!"

"Why?" I demanded.

"My people don't age."

"No way. You look like you're ten years old."

"Not years—centuries." He laughed even harder. "Time moves differently here. With knowledge, we advance to higher levels, and our mental growth is marked in inches. The most advanced elders are over ten feet tall."

"Then how come you're shorter than me?" Lucas asked.

"Because I don't waste time studying." Hank scowled. "That's all everyone wants to do around here. Boring-smoring!"

"Instead you sneak out to play pranks," I accused.

"Yeppers. It was fun."

"Not for the Truelocks."

"I stopped like I promised." Hank grinned. "Now that you're here, I won't be bored anymore. Come on! I'll show you the Imagine Chamber."

Before we could ask more questions, he led us down another corridor. He tapped a plain wooden panel, which dissolved into a doorway.

"It's empty," I said, disappointed as I looked around.

"And dinky," Lucas added. "My closet is bigger."

"That's because you're looking with your eyes." Hank tapped his forehead. "Look with your imagination."

That didn't make any sense, but then nothing had since we'd crossed the bridge into this strange place. So I closed my eyes and visualized walls expanding. I painted them sunshine yellow and put ocean landscape pictures on the walls like in my parents' suite. I'd always wanted a canopy bed, so I added a four-poster bed with a frilly lace canopy and lots of cushy pillows. While I was at it, I threw in a big-screen TV and a hot tub.

When I opened my eyes, I stood in a spacious suite fit for a princess.

"Cool!" Lucas exclaimed. "There's hay and a loft like our barn rooms."

"No way," I argued. "It's a luxurious suite."

"You're nuts, Cassie. Watch out or you'll step into that cow pie."

"And you'll fall in the hot tub."

"You're both right," Hank said smiling.

"How can Lucas and I see two different rooms?"

"Easy," Hank replied. "Whatever you imagine becomes real."

"Then shiver me timbers, I'm going to be a pirate." Lucas sliced with his arm as if he held a sword. "Me mates are waiting for me on a ship with black sails—over there! Yonder waves a skull and crossbones flag."

"Sail away, Captain Lucas," Hank said with a salute.

Instead of imagining something, I thought of someone.

Rosalie.

And there she was. Flipping her thick raven hair from her face as she climbed in from a window that wasn't there a moment ago. She waved and called me over.

I started to go, then stopped. The real Rosalie was over two hundred miles away.

"It's like a virtual-reality game," I said with my eyes wide open. As I spoke, the window faded to an empty wall and Rosalie was gone.

"Pretend is more fun," Hank said.

"But we can't pretend all the time," I argued.

"Why not?" he challenged. "No one here will stop us."

"We can't stay much longer anyway," I told him.

"Cassie's right. It's been cool hanging out, but we better go." Lucas swayed a few feet off the ground from a rope I couldn't see.

"Yeah," I added. "We have to get back to our family."

Hank shook his head. "No, you don't."

"Why not?" Lucas fell as if his rope suddenly snapped in two.

"Because this is your home now." Hank gave us a serious look. "You're going to stay and be my best friends. Forever."

chapter twenty

Play
Grounded

Lucas and I didn't take this news very well. We argued and threatened and pleaded, but Hank stubbornly refused to show us the way out.

While Hank hurried ahead down the corridor, I whispered to Lucas, "Play along so Hank thinks we want to stay."

"But I don't want to. I'll miss my acting classes."

"And I'll miss Rosalie. But it will be harder to sneak away if Hank knows we're plotting to leave. We have to convince him we want to stay."

"I'm not that good of an actor."

"It's our only chance for escape."

"Well . . . I'll try," he said, biting his lip.

"Don't worry, we'll get out of here." I spoke confidently, but inside I was terrified. The farther we traveled underground, the harder it would be to find our way out. I thought of our parents above ground, searching for us. They'd call our names, over and over, but only echoes would reply. And Amber would start to cry.

Swallowing hard, I followed Hank into a room with a log-style bed, a tall, narrow pine dresser, and a shelf where tiny horse statues pranced in a miniature corral. The walls were decorated with rustic paintings of cowboys throwing lassos and wild horses running. And a leather chair shaped like an oversized saddle creaked slightly as it rocked back and forth.

"Well, how do you like my room?" Hank asked proudly.

"It's cool," I said in awe. "The horse statues look real."

"They are. Whenever I want to ride, I shrink down and gallop inside one of the pictures. I always wanted to be a cowboy."

"I was a cowboy last month. But my horse was a broom." Lucas grinned. "So who painted the pictures?"

"Me. I used a trained brush."

"A what?" Lucas asked, sitting on the bed.

"A paintbrush trained by master artists. Why learn to paint when the brush can do the work? While the brush painted, I played in the Arena. It's the best place under earth," he added. "I'll show you tomorrow."

"Tomorrow? Why not now?" I asked.

"Because it's night time."

"It can't be! We didn't even have dinner."

"Are you hungry?"

I started to say "yes," but instead I yawned. Suddenly I was so exhausted I only wanted to sleep. I had no idea what time it was since my wristwatch had stopped at 1:46 PM—as though time ended when we crossed through the waterfall.

Hank offered me his bed, then he set up cots for himself and Lucas.

Jennifer crawled out of my backpack and curled on my pillow. Her purring calmed me as I closed my eyes.

Tomorrow, I vowed. We'll find a way home.

•   •   •

When I awoke, sunshine streamed through a high window in the ceiling. I didn't think it was the real sky, but it was nice.

"Good morning," Hank called out. His cot was folded, and he wore a navy-blue jumpsuit made of fabric that glittered with stars. His black cowboy boots poked out from the pant legs.

Lucas was dressed oddly, too, in a midnight-black jumpsuit.

"I am a magician," Lucas said with a sweep of his arm and a low bow. "Do not mess with me, mortal girl."

I groaned. Lucas the Ham was back.

"You'll need new garments, too," Hank told me.

"No thanks." I covered my T-shirt protectively. "I like my own clothes."

"It'll be easier to fit in if you dress like everyone else."

"What will happen if we're discovered?" I asked, my heart quickening as I remembered Hank's mention of a "Pit."

Hank just shrugged. "My people are peaceful and polite. As long as you don't break rules, no one will bother you. Now hold out your arms, Cassie."

Silky lace sleeves puffed on my shoulders, and a gown woven with tiny diamonds and emeralds flowed around me. The gown's ruffled collar made a good hiding place for Jennifer. She purred as I wrapped her around my neck.

I was too bewildered to protest as Hank led us down a long hall. He made a few turns before stopping at an arched doorway.

"This is the Arena," he told us excitedly.

We entered an amusement park with spinning slides as tall as skyscrapers, fire-breathing-dragon roller coasters, a maze of mirrors where your own reflection mocked you, and even a theater with a closed curtain sweeping across a stage. The only thing missing was other people.

Lucas' face lit up when he saw the theater. "Wow!" was all he could say.

He ran backstage and found props and costumes. He announced that he would act out a skit for us and dashed behind the curtain. After a few minutes, the curtain rose, and I gasped at the amazing scene. It was the inside of a castle at night, complete with torches, eerie fog, and suits of armor. I was impressed.

Then Lucas walked onto the stage, in costume and looking very serious. "To be, or not to be: that is the question: Whether 'tis nobler in the mind to suffer the slings and arrows of outrageous fortune . . ."

Lucas went on for a while, and then suddenly, I just couldn't help it. I giggled and elbowed Hank. "Lucas is wearing tights!"

"*Shh!* He's playing Hamlet. This is a famous scene from Shakespeare."

"Oh." I looked back to the stage, and Lucas was still pacing and talking to himself.

"For who would bear the whips and scorns of time, the oppressor's wrong, the proud man's contumely, the pangs of despised love, the law's delay . . ."

I whispered to Hank, "What's *contumely?*"

"*Shh!* It means rudeness," Hank whispered back.

Lucas went on for a couple more minutes, pacing and rubbing his hands together. I didn't understand half of what he was saying, but he was so convincing and dramatic, I almost forgot he was wearing tights. When he finally finished, Hank and I clapped loudly as Lucas bowed.

Afterward, we explored the mirror maze, bumping into our reflections, who then shouted at us for disturbing them. We shouted back and laughed at ourselves. Time drifted away as we slid and swung and rode thrilling rides. I knew I should be planning our escape, but it seemed less and less important.

We only stopped playing long enough to eat. Hank led us into a room that reminded me of a school cafeteria but fancier. A long table set with plates, silverware, crystal glasses, and candles flickered in welcome. We were the only guests of very peculiar hosts.

"What are they?" I whispered to Hank, trying not to stare at the short, chubby creatures with smiling, pinkish moon faces. They had six long, floppy arms and spinning toes like wheels on their feet. Instead of running, they rolled speedily from table to table as they waited on diners.

"Grubme folk. The elders rescued them from a dying planet. They live for making food and will fix anything we want. They're the best chefs in the universe."

Lucas and I shared an excited look. No more tofu, bean sprouts, or organic casseroles. Junk food here we come!

We enjoyed a main course of strawberry caramel ice cream, with a side dish of French fries, and pizza for dessert. Instead of milk or juice to drink, we slurped strawberry sodas. We pigged out until we were stuffed.

Next stop: the Imagine Chamber. We zoomed away on flying battleships and waged a war of tickle tag. We were each armed with six tickle sticks (like arrows with feathers on the tips). By giving a command of "attack!" our tickle sticks would shoot off after the "enemy" and proceed to tickle relentlessly. Lucas was especially ticklish and doubled over with laughter so hard he had tears in his eyes. Then the guys joined forces and tickle attacked me. Losing a game had never been so fun.

The day lasted so long, it might have been a week. Eventually we grew tired and returned to Hank's room.

Only when we opened Hank's door, it led to a hallway with three different colored doors: blue, brown, and purple.

"Where'd your room go?" Lucas asked Hank.

Hank grinned and pointed to the brown door. "It's in there. The blue door leads to your room."

"Is the purple mine?" I asked eagerly.

"Yeppers. Go ahead and check it out."

I turned the knob and stepped inside a suite fit for a queen. And I felt a bit royal, too, decked out in diamonds and emeralds. I stepped onto soft carpet the color of frosted plums and crossed over to a beautiful canopy bed. The bed was covered with gold and purple satin pillows and a lavender quilt embroidered with prancing unicorns. Also, there was a mirrored vanity and a wardrobe closet full of glittering robes.

Lucas had a cool room, too. It was decorated like a theater, with playbills and posters on the walls. There was a bookshelf packed full of plays and movies, and a crimson velvet canopy draped across the bed like a stage curtain. When he pressed a button to open the curtains, applause burst out. Lucas waved and bowed to his imaginary fans.

"Do you like it?" Hank asked my brother.

"Do I ever! I could stay here forever!"

"That's the idea." Hank turned to me. "What about you, Cassie? Do you like your room?"

My room. Just hearing those words gave me a thrill. Not a room I had to share with Amber, but *my* room. I'd been begging my parents forever for a room of my own. Amber was okay for a sister, but as a roommate, she drove me crazy. She was a total neat freak and complained whenever I left my stuff on the floor.

But I wasn't going to be staying here very long.

"This room is fine," I told Hank. "Everything has been great today."

"And it'll get even better. I have lots of surprises planned." Hank jumped excitedly. "I'm going to arrange one now."

After he left, I turned to Lucas. "Great acting. Hank really thinks you want to stay."

"Well . . ." Lucas plucked a tickle-stick feather from his hair. "It wasn't hard."

"We can sneak away tomorrow. I have a compass and flashlight in my backpack. That should make it easier to escape."

"Why hurry? Hank said we could watch classic movies. And I love the food here." He licked his lips. "Mom never let us have ice cream for dinner."

"Or pizza with thick crust and extra cheese." My mouth watered. "But we shouldn't talk like this."

"Why not?" Lucas raised his eyebrows.

"Being here is changing us. When I think about Mom and Dad, I can't remember their faces. It could be part of the magic of this world—that it confuses our memories. Like the more fun we have, the more we forget our real lives."

"Hank is more fun than anyone I know. He loves movies and Shakespeare, just like I do."

"Yeah, but he's not our family. We have to go home."

"No, we don't."

I dug my fingers into my soft, comfy quilt. "What are you saying?"

"That I like it here." He folded his arms across his chest. "Cassie, I'm not going anywhere. I'm staying."

chapter twenty-one
Maristella

Panic gripped my heart. Lucas couldn't be serious! He wasn't acting like himself. It was as if he'd been enchanted or brainwashed. But not me . . . at least not yet. My memories of Mom, Dad, Amber, and even Rosalie were fuzzy. If I stayed much longer, would they fade away completely? I had to get out of here before that happened. But how could I leave without my brother?

Then stay, a voice whispered in my head.

If I did, I wouldn't have to start a new school in a few weeks. As a lowly sixth grader, I'd be lost in a mob of bigger kids—pushed around, teased, or ignored. I wasn't ready to go to middle school. I preferred elementary school, where I stayed with one teacher all day. Going from teacher to teacher sounded scary. And what if Rosalie wanted to hang out with her new Club Glorious friends?

Deep down, I knew it was wrong to stay—but it was hard to remember why. Something to do with my family. My thoughts were hazy and my feelings confused. I'd decide about leaving tomorrow.

That night, my dreams were peaceful. And I woke up with an idea for a new game.

"You both made treasure maps for me," I told the boys. "Now it's my turn."

"Great!" Hank said as he ran a comb through his mussed hair.

"What's the treasure going to be?" my brother asked.

I touched my chin thoughtfully. What would make a good treasure? Money and jewels weren't valuable here. Even magic was ordinary.

"I know!" I snapped my fingers. "I'll hide an out-of-this-world treasure."

"What?" they asked.

I pointed to the furry alien sleeping on my pillow.

Then I scooped up Jennifer and tucked her under the collar of my robe.

While the boys went to the Arena, I set out to find the perfect hiding place.

Whenever I passed someone in a robe, I tensed. Could they tell I was an outsider? Would they shout out an alarm?

But there were never any shouts—only smiles. Tall or short, the robed people would bow politely then go on their ways. It was so tempting to stay—except forever was a long time to be away from my family.

Regardless of my decision, it would be good to know the way back to the waterfall. And a treasure hunt gave me a chance to explore without Hank getting suspicious.

I made several twists and turns, jotting them down in my notebook. This community had different floors, like a hotel. Instead of rising up to the sky, though, these floors went underground. The Celestial Chamber and Healing Chamber were on the first floor down. The Story Chamber was on the second floor. And the Imagine Chamber, the Arena, the cafeteria, and Hank's room were on the third.

How far down do the floors go? I wondered.

Hank had warned me to stay on the third floor, but when I found a twisty staircase leading to a lower level, I couldn't resist. It was dark except for the fluttering light creatures and odd illuminated symbols that I didn't understand in the rock wall. I went down and down but found no doors. It was like a never-ending tunnel that led to nowhere.

Discouraged, I headed back up.

When I was almost to the top, I paused to study the glowing symbols on the wall. The symbols reminded me of some of the drawings on Hank's map. Wavy lines meant water, right? So I reached out with a shaky hand and touched the wall.

There was beep and the wall shuddered.

"Oh!" I cried, jerking back my hand.

The wall cracked, breaking into a jagged door that slid apart and revealed sunlight outdoors. I smothered my gasp and stared in total amazement at trees, wild grass, mossy rocks, a giant waterfall, and sky.

But how was that possible deep underground?

I was staring so intently, I didn't notice the girl in a pink robe until she stood in front of me. "Greetings," she said, bowing politely.

"Uh . . ." I smiled shyly. "Greetings."

"May I be of any help?" Honey-blond curls framed her heart-shaped face. "You appear lost."

"I can find my way back."

"I do not believe we have met. I am Maristella."

"And I'm Cassie."

"Very honored to meet you. Where do you hail from?"

"Hail? Oh, you mean where do I *come* from. That's kind of hard to explain . . ." I gulped nervously and looked down at my clasped hands.

"I apologize for my rude question," she said with a blush. "Often I speak before thoughts enter my head. This is why I'm only a second level."

"I like to ask questions, too." I relaxed a little. "Is it okay if I ask one?"

"It's against rules, but I won't tell." Dimples formed when she smiled.

"How can we be underground and still see the sky?"

"Paradise is the vortex of all things natural. Earth, sun, moon, and living creatures meet here in harmony."

"How is that possible?"

She giggled. "You ask more questions than I do. I suppose that explains why we are of the same height."

"I guess." I wasn't sure how much I should tell her. I'd never forgotten Hank's mention of a Pit, and I didn't want to get into trouble.

"Come meet my companions," she invited with a wave of her hand. "We have gathered for a picnic. Please join us."

"I can't." I glimpsed a group of robed figures among the trees and moved back toward the doorway. "I'd better go."

"Why?" She tilted her head curiously. "Have I offended you?"

"No! It's just that my brother and a friend are waiting for me."

"Bring them along. All are welcome in Paradise."

"Thanks, but we're in the middle of a game. I have to hide Jennifer."

At the sound of her name, Jennifer poked her head from my collar. I pushed her back, but it was too late.

"Stars above!" Maristella cried, her eyes wide. "They do exist!"

"I can explain—"

"A goofink!" she rejoiced. "I never expected such an honor. May I touch it?"

"Sure." It was still a shock to realize Hank's people knew about goofinks. "Jennifer is friendly."

Maristella reached out. "She is softer than a cloud. And she hums an ancient greeting of her culture. I must study more to learn her language."

"She has a language? I just thought she liked to purr."

"Her language is beautiful. Learning it would put me closer to a higher level. Many of my friends are already third levels," she added enviously.

"You'll get there, too," I encouraged.

"My friends would enjoy seeing the goofink," she said.

"Maybe another time." I shook my head. "I—I really have to go."

"Of course." She sounded disappointed, but never stopped smiling. "Perhaps tomorrow? We could meet here and become better acquainted."

"Uh . . . maybe." I tucked Jennifer back under my collar. "'Bye."

"Farewell, new friend." She gave a deep bow.

I waved, pleased with her words. *New friend*—I liked that.

Still smiling, I left Paradise.

When I reached my floor, I heard my name being called.

"There you are!" Lucas and Hank hurried toward me.

"We've been looking everywhere!" my brother said, sounding relieved. "I was afraid you were lost."

"Why did you leave our floor?" Hank demanded.

"I was exploring, and I made a cool friend."

"Where?"

"Down one level—in Paradise."

Hank gasped. "Why did you go there?"

"I was curious when I found the door. Then I met this girl named Maristella, and she invited me for a picnic. Come with me and meet her. She has other friends, too, and they're all our age—I mean—our height."

But Hank had turned pale. "NO!" he snapped.

"Why not?" Lucas put in. "I'd like to meet Cassie's friend."

"I can't go in there." Hank backed away. "Not ever!"

Then he ran into his room and slammed the door.

chapter twenty-two

Wings and Waterskins

Hank refused to answer any of our questions about Paradise.

"I'll tell you about anything else," he said firmly. "But not that."

"Why?" Lucas and I asked.

"Because it's too personal," he answered. "I can't talk about it."

"Can't or won't?" I challenged.

"Both."

Then he changed the subject, and we spent the rest of the day in the Arena playing games. The treasure hunt was forgotten. But I couldn't forget Maristella.

And even though Hank told me to stay away from Paradise, I returned the next day after Hank and Lucas went to the Arena. Leaving Jennifer in my room, I crept down the staircase and stepped into the impossibly sunny outdoors.

"Cassie!" Maristella's face lit up when she saw me. "I hoped you would come again. I prepared an extra lunch for you."

"Thanks."

"Come over and meet my friends."

"Are you sure they won't mind my being here?" I asked uncertainly.

"Absolutely," she said with so much enthusiasm I couldn't refuse.

Maristella led me over to a picnic table by a sun-sparkled stream where silver fish wiggled in waves. She introduced me to three boys and two girls of my height. They smiled, bowed, and welcomed me like family.

Mostly, they talked about their lessons. Jahrome was studying the stars; Elliot and Bruella shared an interest in history; Zeffry loved ocean studies; and Mayfred wove brilliant designs into delicate fabric stretched on an embroidery hoop. Sometimes, they spoke in languages that sounded strange, yet I understood them. They asked no questions about where I came from, accepting me simply as a friend.

We played an odd game similar to an Easter egg hunt. Only instead of eggs, we searched for tiny creatures called *Boobugs,* and instead of looking on the ground, we searched high in the trees. Boobugs were tucked like baby birds into nests and would bounce away unless you sang to them. They had no eyes, only tiny earflaps and a wide, oblong mouth. Catching them wasn't hard, but when you picked them up, they made rude burping noises.

Maristella chose me first for her Boobug-hunt team. No one kept score, so there were no losers. Maristella loaned me a pair of winged tennis shoes and the ground shrank away as my fluttery feet lifted me high over treetops. I soared along with my new friends, dodging branches and diving over the rushing waterfall. Amazing!

We came down to earth (below earth, I guess) and had lunch—fried chicken nuggets shaped like stars, cucumber slices, and strawberries dipped in cream.

Afterward, everyone raced to the crystal-clear pool by the waterfall.

"Come on, Cassie," Maristella invited, kicking off her shoes. "Let's go swimming."

"I don't have a bathing suit." I ran after her.

"You don't need one. Take off your robe."

"And swim in my underwear?"

"No. Take those off, too."

"Then I'd be naked!" I stopped dead and wrapped my arms around myself. "No way!"

She giggled. "We swim in waterskins."

"I don't think I have one."

"Everyone does. Step into the water, and I'll help you change into yours."

She meant "change" literally. As I stood there, surrounded by natural beauty and unnatural weirdness, I felt a fluttery feeling in my stomach. My skin tingled, and when I looked down, my feet had transformed to a tail and my arms were dark gray fins.

When I saw my reflection in the water, I couldn't believe it. I wasn't human anymore—I was a seal.

Splash! I slid into the deep water and looked around for Maristella. All I saw was a silvery dolphin dancing on its wiggling tail.

"Your seal skin is lovely," the dolphin told me.

"Maristella!" I exclaimed, recognizing my new friend's voice. "Is that you?"

"The answer to that question is obvious," she teased. "Come, let's join the others."

The others were hard to recognize in their water skins: a stingray, a beaver, another dolphin, and even an alligator. We spoke telepathically and stayed underwater for hours, playing games like dive 'n' seek and splash tag. It was amazing to discover I could breathe underwater. In Paradise, everything was possible. I could fly like a bird and swim like a fish. And best of all, I had wonderful new friends.

This was the beginning of many carefree afternoons. While Hank and Lucas filmed movies or rode wild broncos, I played in Paradise. The underground world wrapped around me as snug as a waterskin. It was so glorious, better than any place in the world.

This was my home now.

I was staying.

chapter twenty-three

Question Marked

Hank didn't approve of my going to Paradise, but he didn't stop me. We just didn't talk about it.

What's he afraid of? I wondered. Paradise was beautiful and never boring. Maristella and my other friends were great. So why was Hank avoiding them?

In my previous life—the one I could hardly remember—I would have tried to solve this mystery. But that seemed faraway and unimportant. Being happy was all that mattered.

And I was very happy.

Still, as days of endless fun passed, there were odd moments when I felt something was missing, though I couldn't imagine what. It was like being thirsty in a sea of fresh drinking water. It mostly happened when my friends talked about their studies. They learned art, history, math, science, and languages on a lower floor I'd never been invited to.

"Could I study, too?" I asked one afternoon during lunch.

All conversation stopped. They stared at me as if I'd said a shocking word.

"Cassie, questions are rude," Maristella whispered as she set aside her sandwich and led me away from the picnic table.

"I just wanted to know—"

"Don't ask." She put her finger to her lips. "We are here to relax. That is enough."

"But is it?" I asked. I vaguely remembered complaining about homework and school. Yet now I yearned to know more, to grow taller and smarter. "You've grown an inch since I met you. I want to learn, too."

"It's not allowed, Cassie." Maristella drew me deeper under the shadow of a willow tree. "Please don't say anymore."

"Why not? Every day after our games you go down to your studies, and I return upstairs alone. Why can't I study with you?"

"Don't ruin things," she pleaded.

"What's wrong with asking questions?"

"The questions are not the problem." Maristella frowned. "It's the answers."

"I don't understand."

"That's because you're not from this world."

"You knew all along?" I felt a jolt. "Why didn't you say anything?"

"Questions can lead to unpleasant answers. We all know you're from above ground. But no one would be rude enough to mention it."

"Weren't you curious how I got here?"

"Well—maybe a little." She grinned sheepishly. "But we are peaceful—unlike in the above world where people fight and hate. Here, we mind our own business and question nothing."

"What would happen if you asked me where I came from?"

"Perhaps nothing." She shrugged. "Or the elders might send you to the Pit."

"The Pit!" I choked. "I've heard of it. What is it?"

"That answer would be very unpleasant." She shuddered. "No more questions."

"Then how will I ever learn anything?"

"There is no reason for you to learn. You are a guest in Paradise." Smiling, she took my hand. "Come on, Cassie. Let's go swimming."

• • •

That night, I had dark dreams—of falling forever into a fiery volcano, of screams and torture, of question marks that twisted into a noose and yanked out my tongue so I couldn't ask questions. There were also faces and voices of people I couldn't remember.

When I awoke, I vowed to never ask another question.

And I might have kept that vow.

Except for Jennifer.

chapter twenty-four

Fortunes
Told

The next morning, after another fun day in Paradise, I returned to my room to find that Jennifer was missing.

I searched everywhere—dresser drawers, under the beds, and in my backpack. I even checked the bathroom. Yet there was no sign of her.

I raced down the hall to the Arena and asked the boys if they had Jennifer.

But they shook their heads.

"Don't worry," Hank assured me, adjusting his admiral's hat. "She'll turn up."

"Poor Jennifer." I wrapped my arms around myself. "Being lost is scary."

"Goofinks are afraid of nothing," Hank said.

"But she's so little, and we're her only friends on Earth."

"I'll help find her," my brother offered.

"You can't leave," Hank said, gesturing to a stage set with cameras and flying, winged ships. "We've got to shoot the scene where the pirates storm the cruise ship!"

"Filming can wait." Lucas turned his back on Hank. "My sister needs me."

Then Lucas and I left the Arena. We searched all through the corridors, calling Jennifer's name, over and over. We looked everywhere, but we found no goofink.

"Maybe she's lost on a lower floor," I suggested. "She might have followed me down to Paradise."

"Or she could be upstairs in the Healing Chamber," Lucas added, rubbing his fake pirate's beard. "She liked the bowls."

"But it's risky to go up there."

"Still your wayward tongue, wench. A hearty pirate thrives on risk," Lucas said with a sweep of his feathered hat.

"You're such a ham." I laughed, but I was grateful to have his support.

We started for the upper staircase, but stopped when we heard music. "That's Jennifer!" I said, looking around excitedly. "Where's it coming from?"

"Down there." Lucas pointed to a low door I'd never noticed before. It was too small for a person, but perfect for a goofink.

Kneeling down, I touched an illuminated button and a panel disappeared to reveal a cozy closet. Inside, Jennifer was curled at the peak of a small mountain of diamonds, rubies, and emeralds.

"It's a jewel chamber," I told my brother.

"Another one?" he asked in a bored tone. "Jennifer, get out of there. We'll take you someplace fun."

The goofink didn't move.

"If you come back to my room, Jennifer," I called softly, "I'll let you snack on my hairbrush."

Her large purple eye blinked as if she were trying to tell me something. Then she sprang up and danced to a salsa beat into my arms. As she cuddled against me, I noticed a round crystal in her mouth.

"What's this?" I picked up the tiny crystal and saw silver glitter inside. "A marble?"

"Or a miniature snow globe?" Lucas guessed.

"It's not snow." I held it up toward the lighted ceiling. As I stared, a world of ocean, land, sky, and people swirled into life. "It's like watching a tiny TV."

"Really?" he perked with interest. "Let me see."

Bending close together, we stared into the glittery globe.

Images spun at a dizzying speed, then slowed as a girl came into focus. She sat at the edge of a swimming pool, her long black braid dangling over the water. She wore a leopard-print swimming suit and looked sad. Strange feelings came over me as I watched her walk over to a group of girls lounging in the sun.

"Rosalie," I murmured as flashes of memory came back. Long talks, sleepovers, giggling over funny movies. Rosalie—my best friend.

And I could hear her voice!

"I'm sick of swimming." She flipped her braid over her shoulders as she sat on a towel. "And it's too hot to play tennis or miniature golf."

"So what do you want to do?" a tall girl with knobby knees asked. "We could talk to Marc Lynburn again."

"He'd just tell us to get lost," Rosalie said.

"I'd get lost with him anytime." A girl with frizzy black hair pulled back in a blue scrunchie sighed. "He's *sooo* cute."

"And he has a dozen girlfriends older than us," Rosalie added. "I'm bored. I wish my friend Cassie were here—she always knows fun things to do. Once we created a cardboard town with real fake money and another time we went on a scavenger hunt for things beginning with the letter *P.* She borrowed a pony and won the game."

"Are you sure this Cassie is real?" Knobby Knees teased. "You keep talking about her, but we've never met her."

"She's on vacation. She's having so much fun, I bet she may never come back." Rosalie slumped on her towel. "I miss her."

"And I miss you, too," I whispered as the picture faded back to silver dust.

The globe turned cold and clouded over. Rosalie was gone.

When I looked at my brother, his lower lip trembled.

"What did you see?" I gently touched his arm.

"A theater on Broadway with my name up in lights. I saw myself years older—bowing and receiving flowers on my opening night. Ms. Bennett was clapping from the audience. It's the future, I think—only how can it happen when I'm here?"

"I think Jennifer led us here so we'd remember what's important. Not fancy clothes and my own room," I said sadly.

"Or making action movies in the Arena," Lucas added.

I sighed. "I'd forgotten so much. It's as if being here put on a spell on me. But it's all coming back now—Rosalie, Mom, Dad, and Amber."

"I want to go home," Lucas said.

"Me too."

"But how can we? Hank will never show us the way out."

"And my friends are too busy minding their own business to help," I said.

"So what are we going to do?"

"Either stay here forever," I clutched the crystal globe, "or find a way out ourselves."

chapter twenty-five
Dead Ends

While Lucas kept Hank busy in the Arena the next day, I snooped around. I used my notebook to map out the passageways. When I knew every corner of our floor, I climbed up to the next one. My heart pounded as I crept through the halls, searching for an escape route.

Down the corridor beyond the Celestial Chamber, I found a junction where four passages branched off into unknown darkness. No light creatures lit these passages, so I couldn't go any farther.

"I'll take my flashlight next time," I told my brother later when Hank was in the bathroom. I opened my notebook and pointed to the drawings I'd made. "One of these passages has to lead to the waterfall."

"I hope so," Lucas said with an uneasy glance at the bathroom door. "I think Hank is getting suspicious."

"How come?"

"He's been giving me weird looks. Like he doesn't trust me."

"Be careful," I warned. "If he finds out our plans, he'll try to stop us."

"Don't worry. I can fool anyone," Lucas said confidently.

"But for how long?" I closed my notebook and hugged it to my chest. "We better check out the passages and escape soon."

Lucas frowned. "How soon?"

"Tonight," I said solemnly. "After Hank falls asleep."

• • •

We left a goodbye note and our robes for Hank to find in the morning. Even though my jeans and T-shirt were wrinkled, it felt good to wear them—like I was myself again.

As I led Lucas up the staircase, I felt the rumble of Jennifer's contented purring from the backpack strapped over my shoulders.

"Which way do we go?" Lucas asked when we reached the upper floor.

"Down this hall and turn right," I whispered.

"It's so quiet," he said with a shiver. "I hope this is the way out."

"Me too."

I tried to sound confident, but I was afraid. So many things could go wrong. Even if we made it across the waterfall bridge, how would we get home? We'd been gone for a long time. Search parties would have given up days ago. We'd have to hike for miles in the dark through the wilderness, where dangerous animals lurked.

But we kept going. We left the halls lit by fluttering light creatures and were plunged into darkness. I snapped on my flashlight.

When we reached the four passages, we tried the one on the far right first. It was a short trip because after about twenty feet we bumped into a rock wall. The next passage went twice as far before we hit a dead end. And the third passage didn't end, but dropped off at a sheer cliff.

"Whoa!" Lucas jumped back with me. "One more step and we would have been goners. Close call!"

I nodded, breathing so hard I couldn't speak. I shined the flashlight into vast nothingness that stretched high above and plunged down for what seemed like forever. Was this the Pit that Hank and Maristella warned me about?

Shivering, I turned around and doubled back. As I reached the main passage, my foot slipped on a pebble. Stumbling, my arms flailed, and I clutched the rocky wall to steady myself. Jennifer squeaked a protest from within my backpack.

"You have too much to carry," Lucas said, coming up beside me. "Let me help."

"That would be great." I reached up to remove my backpack, only Lucas grabbed my flashlight instead.

"I'll carry this," he offered.

"Gee, thanks," I said sarcastically.

"You're welcome." He grinned, aiming the bright beam into the fourth passage. "I'll lead the way."

"Hold the flashlight steady," I told him.

"I am," Lucas insisted.

"Then why is it flickering?"

"I don't know. The batteries must be—" His voice broke off as we were plunged into total blackness. "Dead."

"Oh, no!" I reached out into the dark. "Lucas, where are you?"

"Here." His hand clasped mine. "This is so freaky. You're standing right here, but I can't see you."

"I can't see either of us." Panic rose in me. "Which way do we go? If there's another cliff, we won't see it. What are we going to do?"

"Come back where you belong," an unexpected voice rang out.

Glaring bright light was as blinding as darkness. Blinking, I whirled around and, as my eyes adjusted, saw Hank holding a lantern.

"Game over," he said bitterly. "I win."

"This isn't a game," I retorted. "And you know it."

"You shouldn't have tried to leave. Come on back." He gestured for us to follow him.

"No, Hank." Lucas shook his head. "We've had a lot of fun. But we're going home."

"You'll never find the way out without my help."

"Then help us," I said quietly.

He snorted. "Not a chance."

Lucas looked pleadingly at Hank. "Hey, we're friends. Aren't we?"

"Yeah. That's why I don't want you to leave."

"But friends help each other," Lucas said in a solemn tone. "And we need your help so we can go home."

"It was boring before you came. No one here knows how to have fun."

"Yes, they do," I argued. "Maristella, Jahrome, Bruella, and my other friends are cool. We swim and fly and play games in Paradise. Why won't you join them?"

"Forget it." He stomped his foot, causing the lantern to sway and shadows to waver across the rock walls. "I'm never going back there."

"What are you afraid of?"

"I never said I was afraid. I just don't—don't fit in." He frowned. "They're all growing taller . . . and I'm still short. They don't even notice me."

He looked away, but not before I saw the shame in his eyes.

And I understood. I felt the same way about going to middle school. Being shorter and younger was scary. But running away wasn't the answer.

Is there an answer? I wondered. Or only unpleasant questions?

Then an idea hit me.

"Hank," I exclaimed. "I think I know the answer to all of our problems."

"What?" He arched an eyebrow skeptically.

"If I can help you become the most popular person in Paradise, will you help us go home?"

He looked doubtful but eventually agreed.

Tomorrow, I thought, I'll create my own kind of magic.

chapter twenty-six

The Secret Weapon

The next morning, Hank argued every step down the stairway to Paradise. "This is a bad idea. Let's try tomorrow. No one will even talk to me. This won't work."

But Lucas and I refused to let him turn back. We literally pushed Hank through the doorway into Paradise.

"Hi, Cassie!" Maristella came toward me. She paused when she noticed the boys, then bowed politely. "I am honored to meet your friends."

"This is my brother, Lucas," I introduced. "And you already know Hank."

"I'm sorry." She shook her head "He is not familiar to me."

"See! She doesn't even recognize me," Hank said angrily. "I told you this wouldn't work."

"Let me talk to her." While Lucas kept a close watch on Hank, I pulled Maristella aside.

"Hank feels left out," I explained. "He played pranks above ground because he was lonely and wanted attention. When that didn't work, he tricked my brother and me into coming here so he'd have friends."

"We are all friends in Paradise."

"But you don't even remember him."

She shrugged. "I am sorry he felt bad, but no one asked him to stay away."

"Or noticed he was gone," I accused. "Friendship means caring enough to ask the hard questions— like, is something wrong? Are you okay? What can I do to help?"

"Questions are rude."

"Not these kind of questions. Where I come from, friends watch out for each other, even if that means asking tough questions."

Maristella frowned. "You say confusing things, Cassie."

"I'm just telling you how I feel . . . even if you're too polite to ask."

"I cannot break rules. But you have given me much to think about."

"Does that mean you'll help Hank?" I asked hopefully.

"Another question!" She gave a hesitant smile. "But the answer is yes."

I smiled back—then told her my idea.

Minutes later, Maristella called everyone over to the picnic area. Hank looked ready to bolt when Jahrome, Elliot, Bruella, Zeffry, and Mayfred gathered around us. No one asked impolite questions, but there was a curious silence.

Maristella bowed respectfully, then gestured to my brother and Hank.

"Please welcome Lucas and Hank."

The others bowed and offered greetings.

"Hank's formal name is Hanniscorn," I added. "He used to play here. Do you remember him?"

They shook their heads, clearly uncomfortable with my question.

"I might as well be invisible," Hank said bitterly. He jumped from the table and started to leave. But he only got a few feet before Lucas grabbed him by the collar.

"Wait," Lucas said firmly. "Give them a chance to get to know you."

"Why bother? They'll forget me when they study."

"So study with them," I suggested.

"Learning is boring. Nothing interests me."

"But that's not true!" I snapped my fingers. "You're interested in maps. You drew amazing pictures and clues on your treasure map."

"Yeah," Lucas agreed. "It was a clever map. If you studied art and geography, you could decipher clues to search for real lost treasures."

"You could map out this world," I added. "And other worlds, too."

Hank stopped struggling and stared at us. "I—I never thought of that."

"Learning new things is exciting," Lucas said.

"Well, I do like treasure hunts. Maybe I could study—a little, anyway."

"Great!" Lucas high-fived Hank. "You'll grow taller in no time."

"And become so popular no one will ever forget you again," I added with a glance at my backpack. "Ready for our secret weapon?"

"Yeppers," Hank said.

Then I unzipped my backpack and lifted out Jennifer.

chapter twenty-seven
Pit Fall

Imagine bringing a live unicorn to school for show 'n' tell.

That's the reaction Hank got when he showed off Jennifer.

Everyone gasped in delight and crowded around Hank. One bold person even asked the question, "May I pet the goofink?" And no one called him rude.

Jennifer loved the attention. She purred joyfully and hip-hopped on her springy tail. Then she bowed her head so everyone had a turn stroking her silky fur.

Afterward, I took Maristella aside and we walked over to the waterfall. With sunlight shining rainbows in the water and a sweet breeze tickling my skin, I confided to Maristella that I would be leaving soon.

Her brows rose in question and she frowned. "It is not wise to go without permission."

"If I stay any longer, my memories will fade again, and I may never find my way back to my family."

"I do not understand about family, but I care about my friends." She reached out for my hand. "I want you to be happy."

"You too." My heart twisted, and for a second, I was tempted to say I would stay. Instead I squeezed her hand. "I won't forget you. You'll always be a special friend."

"Friends always," she said.

Impulsively, I reached into my pocket and pulled out a velvet pouch. I gave it to Maristella. "I want you to have this."

She opened the pouch and her face lit up when she held the tiny rose quartz cat. "It's beautiful," she murmured in awe. "A very precious treasure. I love it!"

I smiled to myself. In a magical world abundant in riches, Maristella saw value in an inexpensive trinket. I guess real value wasn't measured in dollars but in special moments like this. I felt a bit taller with understanding.

"Thank you," Maristella said humbly. "Only I have no gift to give you."

"You've given me more than you know. But there is something you can do for me."

Then I explained to Maristella, who had been studying the Goofink language, that I needed to ask Jennifer an important question. This question wasn't rude, but the answer made me sad.

Yes, Jennifer would rather stay with Hank. She loved being underground in a magical world that reminded her of home. I knew she'd be happier here, but I hadn't known how hard it would be saying goodbye.

When I hugged her for the last time, a lump filled my throat.

My hand shook as I gave her a farewell gift: a few strands of my hair.

• • •

Hank kept his word, and after one last magical day in Paradise, he led Lucas and me to the upper floor. We followed the same route that ended at the four dark passages. But instead of going to the fourth, unexplored tunnel as I'd expected, he pointed to the third tunnel.

"But we already tried this way," I said anxiously. "It ends at a cliff."

"That's the Pit," Hank said calmly.

"No way!" I gasped. "Why'd you bring us here?"

"Are you trying to kill us?" Lucas accused.

Hank lifted his lantern high and gestured for us to follow him. "You'll be safe."

My heart pounded. "But everyone is afraid of the Pit."

"And they should be." His tone was serious, but his golden eyes twinkled. "It leads to a dangerous place."

"Where?" Lucas asked.

"Above ground."

I stared at Hank in bewilderment. "But that's *our* world."

Hank smirked. "Well, your world is scary."

"Only when you're around playing pranks," I teased.

"But I promised to stop playing pranks, and I will—at least in your world. This one could use a little shaking up, though."

"The elders better watch out for Earthquake Hank," I joked. Then I glanced uneasily into the dark passage ahead. "Will you lead us back to the resort?"

"Sorry, but I can't." Hank shook his head. "From now on, I'm playing by the rules. And that means not going above ground."

"So how will we get home?" I asked.

"Home will find you."

"What's that supposed to mean?" A chilly breeze blew from deep within the tunnel and goosebumps rose on my bare arms.

"You'll see," Hank said with a sly snicker.

"I guess this is goodbye," Lucas said sadly. "Thanks for all the stories and plays and battles. It's been great."

"Better than great. It's been—"

I grinned at Lucas and we both said together, "Neato mosquito!"

We all laughed, but then we grew silent. It had been fun to be with Hank, and Lucas and I both knew we'd miss him.

Hank sniffled a bit, and then he stiffened. "Boring-smoring! Enough goodbyes!" He faced us as Lucas and I stood with our backs to the cliff. "In the words of a fellow prankster, 'Give me your hands, if we be friends, and Robin shall restore amends.'"

"Who's Robin?" I wasn't sure what he was talking about but Hank winked at Lucas, and Lucas smiled like he understood.

Then Hank took my hand and Lucas'. "So how does this work, Hank? Does a bridge appear?" I asked.

Hank shook his head and smiled mischievously. Then he pushed us over the cliff.

chapter twenty-eight
Miles and Minutes

Everything went hazy after that. I don't remember falling, but I remember landing with a hard thump on rough ground. And when my head cleared, I saw a bright sun overhead and heard the soft rushing of water. Thick forest seemed to crowd around like an audience waiting to see what would happen next.

"Lucas!" I cried, spotting my brother lying a few feet away.

"Are we out?" He rubbed his eyes and stood up shakily.

"I think so. Only it's not night anymore."

"We must have been knocked out for a long time."

"Look." I glanced at my arm with a gasp. "My watch is working again!"

"Guess that proves we're back. But where are we?"

I climbed on a tall rock and saw trees climbing up tall mountains, jutting rocks, and a grassy meadow with a stream snaking through it. "That's the meadow where you found me."

"Then we're not far from the parking lot," he said excitedly. "Let's hurry!"

"For what?" I asked, sinking down on the rock. "We've been gone for almost two weeks. No one will be waiting for us."

"Oh." Lucas slumped beside me. "I forgot."

"Everyone must think we're lost—or worse." I shuddered. "The search parties would have given up days ago. Mom, Dad, and Amber would have gone back home."

"Over two hundred miles away." His shoulders sagged. "How do we get there?"

"Find someone to help," I reassured, giving him a pat on the shoulder. He may be a whiz kid, but he was still my little brother. "Let's check the parking lot for a ranger or a nice tourist family. We made it this far, what's another two hundred miles?"

He gave a weak smile; then we started walking. We found a trail and followed it through the meadow, over a small hill, around rocks and bushes, until we came to a hilly spot overlooking the parking lot.

Then we stared, too shocked to utter a word. There wasn't a ranger truck, but there was a van with a nice—very familiar—family having lunch on a picnic table.

With whoops of joy, Lucas and I raced to Mom, Dad, and Amber.

chapter twenty-nine

Too Strange

I opened my arms ready for hugs and tears, but there was no happy reunion.

Dad munched on wheat-germ chips without looking at us. Amber noisily slurped wheat-grass juice through a straw. And Mom set down her eggplant and arugula sandwich and glanced up.

"Did you find the stream?" Mom asked calmly.

"What? No—I mean, yes," I stammered in shock. "Is that all you can ask?"

"Didn't you miss us?" Lucas demanded.

"Not really," Mom said as she handed a napkin to Amber, who had jelly smeared on her nose.

"But we were far away and couldn't get back!" I exclaimed.

Lucas nodded. "We were gone for a long time."

"Oh, really?" Dad chuckled and glanced at his wristwatch. "It's only been five minutes since Cassie left to wash her hands."

I leaned against the table weakly. "But that's impossible!"

There was the sound of another car approaching and a sleek black SUV parked next to us. Lucas stared in astonishment at Trevor and his father.

That's when we both realized the weird truth.

The days we'd spent with Hank underground didn't exist here. Hank was right about time moving differently. It went backward! I checked my watched and saw that it was 1:30—only minutes after my family came to Panther Meadows. Lucas and I had returned before we'd even left—which was confusing. No one would believe us if we told the truth, so we kept quiet and tried to act normal.

But a few hours later, things got even more confusing when we returned to the Golden Shamrock Resort.

Mrs. Truelock ran out to meet our van. I had a feeling she'd been watching for us. Her face was flushed and blue-gray hairs dangled from her upswept bun. Something was definitely wrong.

"I'm so glad you're back," she cried, pausing to catch her breath. "There's been another prank."

Dad stepped out of the van. "What happened?"

"Look for yourself!" She pointed to the barn, where someone had painted a giant pot of gold. "Right after you left this morning, the leprechaun left that message."

As I moved closer, I read the scrawled words under the picture. "Come for my gold tonight, when the moon glows bright."

"It's a challenge," Dad said with a glint in his eyes. "And I accept."

"Be careful," Mrs. Truelock warned. "There's no telling what that little fellow can do. When my husband caught him painting the barn, the little monster cast a spell that paralyzed my husband. Then, bold as day, he pranced around in gold slippers and a pointy green hat. He laughed in this shrill way that gave me shivers. And my poor husband was frozen stiff until the prankster flew off into those trees."

"But that's impossible," I whispered to Lucas. "Hank was with us."

"And he'd never wear gold slippers," my brother added.

"So who's the prankster?" I wondered.

"I think I know." Lucas pursed his lips and stared off at the resort. "And I've got an idea how to prove it."

chapter thirty
Role Call

Dad's TV crew was in place as a slice of moon rose high into a dark sky. Night temperatures had dropped sharply and everyone wore heavy coats, hats, and mittens. Producer Monica Dumano shouted orders, and cameraman Fred obeyed with a patient grin. Dad checked his cordless mike and paced back and forth.

Lucas and I ducked down behind the barn. Mr. and Mrs. Truelock watched from the darkened front porch of the resort with several guests. No one wanted to miss out on the excitement.

"It's nearly midnight," Dad called out in a low whisper. "Take your positions and quiet, everyone."

Lucas nudged me. "That's my cue to go."

"Where?" I demanded, annoyed that he hadn't explained his plan.

"To make a phone call."

"This late at night? Who are you calling?"

He grinned and turned without answering.

As he headed for the main building, there was a sudden commotion from the opposite direction. When I looked into the woods, green lights flickered through shadowy trees like dancing fairies. Irish music floated through the darkness, and the green lights grew brighter.

There was a rustle of footsteps and hushed voices as Dad's crew sprang into position. They were using an infrared camera to film at night and high-tech sound equipment. My heart quickened, and I crossed my fingers.

A small, red-haired figure dressed in green pranced out of the trees. His golden skin glowed, and his wide mouth twisted into a grotesque grin. He waved a crock of gold in the air. "Catch me if you can!" he shouted.

"Who are you?" Dad stepped forward, but his crew remained hidden in shadows.

"Wouldn't you like to know?" The leprechaun laughed shrilly.

"Come closer so we can talk better," Dad said.

"Stay back!" The little guy shouted, springing into a high jump. "Or I'll vanish, and you'll never get me gold!"

"I don't want your gold. I just want to talk with you." Dad took a few steps forward.

"I said no closer! Or I'll turn you into a lizard!"

"I'm impressed. Only someone very powerful could do such incredible magic." Dad sounded serious, but I could tell it was all an act. He didn't believe in leprechauns or magic. He was just waiting for the right moment to unmask the little imposter.

But what if he wasn't an imposter? I worried. What if the prankster *was* Hank or one of his friends in disguise? The prankster was the same size as Hank. And, after all, only someone from a magical world could freeze Mr. Truelock or fly through the air.

"Yes, I'm very powerful," the leprechaun boasted in a voice that suddenly sounded vaguely familiar. "So don't mess with me."

"I only want to know what you want," Dad called out in a friendly tone. "Why do you play pranks?"

"To protect me golden crock."

"That doesn't look like real gold to me," Dad said. "Just painted rocks."

"All leprechauns have gold," the prankster exclaimed. "My gold is the source of my power and with it, I can do anything."

"Then prove it. Show me some magic," Dad said, inching forward. I could hear the whirl of cameras and knew Fred was getting this all on tape.

"Don't come any closer!" A green hand rose in warning. "You can't trick me into giving you my gold. I'm going to fly—"

"NO!" a shout erupted from a familiar blond man. He rushed past Dad and grabbed the leprechaun by the arm. "You're coming with me!"

It was Mr. Tremaine.

"What do you think you're doing?" the lep-rechaun shouted, his Irish accent suddenly gone. "Let go!"

"There isn't time for arguments," Mr. Tremaine said angrily. Then he yanked off the green cap and a red wig.

"Trevor!" I exclaimed, jumping up.

"Dad, how could you?" Trevor stomped his golden slippers. "You know better than to interfere when I'm working."

"Come along and get out of that ridiculous cos-tume," Mr. Tremaine said impatiently. "I'll explain everything in the car."

"Not until you explain all this to us." Dad stepped between them. "What's going on?"

"Ask him!" Mr. Tremaine pointed to Mr. Truelock. "He hired my son to pose as a leprechaun. This whole farce is his doing!"

All eyes turned to the elderly resort owner.

"Walter, is he telling the truth?" Mrs. Truelock asked with a sob.

"I'm sorry, Sugarkins." Her husband hung his shaggy head in shame. "But I did it to help improve business."

"Help?" she shrieked. "By scaring the guests and ruining the rooms?"

"I didn't have anything to do with those pranks."

"But you hired an actor to play a leprechaun?"

"Only after I saw how our leprechaun made the newspapers and gained the attention of a TV show. I realized this was our chance for fame. But I wanted to make sure Mr. Strange had something to film, so I hired Trevor."

"And I fooled all of you," Trevor bragged. "Until my dad butted in." He glared at his father.

"But I had to, Trev," his father said excitedly. "We got The Call."

"No way! From Leon?" Trevor's eyes almost bugged out.

"Yes! Leon's assistant tracked you down and wants you to audition tomorrow afternoon in LA for a starring role in a Goldstone movie."

"So why are we wasting time here?" Trevor grabbed his father's hand. "Let's hit the road."

No one stopped them from leaving. They hadn't committed any crime—not exactly. And Dad's crew was busy interviewing the Truelocks. They filmed the fake red wig, and Mr. Truelock explained how he rigged a rope in the trees so it made it appear that Trevor was flying. He couldn't explain about the fish in the pool or the shoes hung from the tree, but no one seemed to care.

As the filming wrapped up, Dad faced the camera with a smile and finished with his trademark phrase, "And that's why I don't believe it."

chapter thirty-one

Home
Glorious

Lucas and I didn't get a chance to talk privately until the next morning when I was packing to leave.

"Lots of surprises last night," I said with a smile. "Isn't that right, Leon?"

"It worked, didn't it?" He chuckled. "I almost feel guilty for tricking Trevor. But he's such a pest, and he kept bragging about getting a role in a Goldstone movie. Who knows? He may get the part."

"And once Dad airs his show, Trevor will be even more famous. I'll bet this resort becomes famous, too," I added.

"It probably will," Lucas agreed. "Visitors will book months in advance to stay in this barn."

"They can have it." I laughed. "I'm ready to go back home and see Rosalie."

"Or you could just look in your crystal globe."

I shook my head. "I've tried it a few times, but it doesn't work anymore."

"Maybe it only works in Hank's world," Lucas guessed.

"Maybe," I said as I finished putting my clothes in my suitcase.

But I had a feeling the magic wasn't over yet.

It was just beginning.

• • •

On the long ride home, I stared out the window. I felt a little sad to leave Mount Shasta, Hank, Maristella, and Jennifer. But I couldn't wait to see Rosalie.

I always thought she was the one who came up with the best ideas, but she'd told her Club Glorious friends that I had good ideas. Maybe we were both right. Being best friends gave us the best ideas when we were together. That was more important than a fancy club.

But would we be together much when I got home? She still belonged to Club Glorious, and my parents hadn't changed their minds about joining. Sure, I could get a guest pass and visit once or twice. But I'd still be left out—unless I could bring the Glorious Girls to me.

If I could help Hank make friends, maybe I could help myself, too.

By the time we reached home, I had a notebook full of ideas.

I raced for the phone and called Rosalie. When she heard my voice, she squealed, "You're back! I'm on my way over!"

Then we planned together every day for a week until it was P-Day: Party Day.

Five girls—plus Rosalie—arrived at my house for a "Treasure Hunt" party. Lucas created the maps, Rosalie and I bought prizes, and Mom made her yummiest healthy snacks.

We split into teams and spent hours following clues. Lucas did a great job with the maps—sometimes it came in handy to have a whiz-kid brother. And when all the prizes were found, we plopped in a video and snacked on popcorn and fruit juices in the family room.

It was glorious! Like having Paradise at home.

Then, midway through the movie, we ran out of popcorn, and I jumped up to go make more.

As I passed Dad's study, I heard him talking on the phone. Something about his tone made me stop and eavesdrop. When he hung up, he noticed me standing in the doorway.

"So you heard?" he asked in a solemn tone.

I gulped and nodded.

"What do you think? This could turn out to be my most thrilling show ever. Should we start planning another family trip?"

"I don't want to leave Rosalie again," I told him.

"So bring her along!" Dad grinned.

"Really?!"

He nodded.

"That would be great!"

"Then I'll start making plans. In two weeks, we're going to see a mermaid."